DOUBLE FEAR

A woman's scream.

Then, Gunn heard the snarl of a cougar.

Another scream, this one high pitched, full of stark terror.

He heard the cat spit and hiss, evidently cornered with the two women.

"Don't move!" he ordered with a hush, entering the adobe in a half-crouch position. With a snarl, the cougar raced two steps and took to the air. It came at Gunn, claws extended, jaws open wide, fangs glistening a dull white in the darkness.

Gunn dropped to the earthen floor, bringing the rifle up defensively. He felt a rush of air pass his face and rammed the rifle snout into the animal's side, pulling the trigger. The smell of black powder permeated the adobe. The cat screamed in pain and rolled over to die. The horses outside were whinnying and stamping. Gunn led the two women from the adobe. Janice held onto him. Amity stayed close.

"Thank you," whispered Janice. "I thought we were going to be eaten alive by that animal."

In the faint light, her eyes were misty, her lips wet. Gunn turned away from her, shocked at the look of raw desire in her eyes.

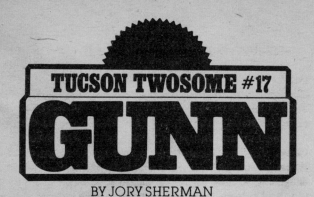

TUCSON TWOSOME #17

GUNN

BY JORY SHERMAN

ZEBRA BOOKS
KENSINGTON PUBLISHING CORP.

ZEBRA BOOKS

are published by

KENSINGTON PUBLISHING CORP.
475 Park Avenue South
New York, N.Y. 10016

Printed in the United States of America

*This one's for
Kathryn Fanning*

CHAPTER ONE

The heat was like an iron mask fired to cherry red in a blacksmith's furnace then laid against a man's skin. The savage fire of noon pressed into the rider's flesh, saturating every pore with the searing venom of raw chili peppers and scalding sand.

The sun scorched the land, the rocks, the dirt, the awesome emptiness, and there was no shade for anything bigger than a lizard. The ocotillo withered and shrank under the blaze of this molten summer day. Even the swollen Gila monsters sought shade under rocks that would fry them like bacon if they ventured atop; the baked granite stones scintillated in the dazzling furnace light.

The sun's hot fist hammered down on the land and the man who rode the big Tennessee Walker sorrel. The sun burned through his dust-caked eyelids and drew moisture out of his cracked, parched lips. The sun's relentless, deadly rays baked his clothes iron hot and sucked at his mind until its fluids were mud dried to a cracked and senseless desert.

The horse had thrown its iron shoes, and the blistering sands seared its hooves. The animal winced as it picked its way toward the valley lying somewhere beyond the shimmering heat waves that made the land dance, made elusive lakes appear and disappear in bewildering succession. Sweat glistened in streaks on the sorrel's hide, and flies gouged holes in its flesh, drinking fresh blood from the open wounds. The horse's tail flicked at its haunches with mindless regularity and the heat rose up from the ground in suffocating waves.

"At least," the man thought, "I have given the Apaches the slip."

For three days he had been chased in a running gun battle by a half dozen Mescalero Apaches. They ran him in relays, two at a time. Esquire, his horse, had thrown the first shoe two days before. The other shoes had been lost sometime yesterday. He didn't know exactly when. The Apaches had not given him much time to think. He had shot one, finally, and winged another, but the other four had run him out into the hell of those blinding white sands until his canteen had run dry. During the night, he had slipped away from them, headed south. But the Rio Grande was too far that way. He'd have to ride almost to El Paso to find it.

Now, riding west toward Mesilla, he figured the Mescaleros had given up on him. He could smell water and Esquire was getting some frisk in his sore-footed gait.

This was a hell of a place for a man without water to be.

But a man on the run from the law sometimes didn't have much of a choice.

Gunn was such a man.

The Apache rose up off the ground twenty yards to the left.

His screams chilled Gunn's blood, and startled Esquire. Esquire reared up on his hind legs, forelegs clawing the air.

Gunn fought him down. The Apache charged, brandishing a tomahawk. He raced across rocky, ocotillo-dotted ground, his painted face adding to the horror of the surprise.

One minute there had been no sign of life. The *rio* lay just beyond where the Apache had appeared. Gunn had meant to ford there.

The hackles rose on the back of Gunn's neck. But he was not fooled. He jerked his pistol from its holster, wheeled Esquire and dug straight, rowelless spurs into the horse's flanks.

The Apache was only a diversion.

Gunn turned his back on the charging brave and swung his pistol, looking for the other three.

Esquire leaped over a mass of stones and broke at an angle leading away from the Apache on foot.

A rifle cracked.

Close by.

The bullet sizzled over Gunn's head, sending shivers down his spine.

The shooter was invisible. Gunn saw the puff of white smoke rising like a miniature cloud in the breezeless air. Below it, nothing. Only rocks and the little yellow-flowered agave they called *lechuguilla* and the narrow-leafed sotol and withered yucca standing like the skeletons of conquistador's spears.

From another direction, another rifle shot. Booming so close his ear drums throbbed with the percussion. This time, orange flame and white smoke.

But no sign of the shooter.

Only the bleak emptiness of the Chihuahuan desert baking in the merciless sun.

The whine of the bullet as it fried a path past Gunn's ear.

Gunn laid the reins over, pulling the bit in Esquire's

mouth. The horse twisted into a turn. Gunn whipped the reins again, to the other side of Esquire's neck and began the zigzag pattern. He charged toward the last puff of smoke as it turned to gauze and floated upward.

He yelled and spurred the horse into a hard run. He felt its energy beneath him, the powerful muscles working, the hooves struggling for purchase on the uneven ground. He looked for movement, a patch of color, anything different, alien.

His yell carried to the river and died on the flats beyond, but the Apaches rose up from the scorched earth and swung rifles, searching for their swerving target. Gunn saw the first one—his face painted black, white, and vermilion—brace himself and bring the rifle to his shoulder. Esquire, responding to the pressure on the bit, changed course and bore down on the brave.

Gunn ducked, leaned over the side of his saddle, and took aim with the pistol. He cocked the trigger, then squeezed. The .45 Colt bucked in his hand. At twenty-five yards he was sure of his mark.

The lead ball slammed into the Apache's chest. After several spasms, the Indian threw up his hands. The rifle flew into the air, twisting lazily before crashing to the ground. The buck staggered and clawed at the hole in his chest. Blood gushed over his fingers. He sucked in air, strangled on blood. A hole in his back flowed crimson. He looked up at the sky and crumpled, his legs collapsing. He twitched, his mouth sucking in sand as he tried to breathe into blood-filled lungs.

The second Apache fired at Gunn from sixty yards.

Gunn sat up straight and wheeled Esquire into a tight turn. The movement saved him. The rifle bullet whizzed past the horse's chest and thunked into an ocotillo, rattling its leaves.

The Apache with the tomahawk disappeared into thin air.

Gunn twisted in the saddle for a shot at the warrior with the rifle. He squeezed off a shot, but knew it would miss. The Apache darted to the left and Gunn tracked him with the pistol. He fired again. Dust kicked up between the Apache's legs. The Indian howled as the grit stung his flesh. He stopped, dropped to his knees and jacked another shell into the chamber of the Winchester.

Gunn rammed hard spurs into Esquire's flanks and heeled the horse over. He leaned back and fired his pistol, sure now of his aim.

Smoke blossomed from the rifle barrel. Orange flame spouted behind the ball. The Apache jerked as the pistol ball crunched into his shoulder. A cry of pain screeched from his throat. The ball shattered the shoulder socket, splintering bone, ripping into tendons and veins. Blood flowed over the brave's chest like a blossoming flower.

Gunn hauled in on the reins as Esquire threatened to overrun the stricken brave. The horse skidded up short, its muscles bundling under the strain. The Apache looked up at the white man with pain-glazed eyes.

He tried to work the rifle, but his left arm hung uselessly from torn muscles and shattered bones.

Gunn drew a breath and stared at his defeated enemy. A muscle twitched in his jaw. His blue gray eyes flickered with shadows. Calmly, he opened the gate on his pistol, worked the ejector lever, and pushed the empty hulls into his palm. He put the empty cartridges into his shirt pocket, pulled bullets from his gun belt, and fitted them into the empty cylinder holes.

He closed the gate and spun the cylinder. He looked at the wounded Apache, his thumb flicking over the

11

hammer as if he was considering whether to cock the pistol or holster it.

"You'll bleed to death or you'll live," he said, "but your fighting's over this day."

The Apache muttered a guttural curse, his dark eyes flashing a hatred that blotted out the pain.

Gunn holstered the Colt, kicked Esquire's flanks, and began searching for the first Apache. As he rode off, he jerked the Winchester from its scabbard and levered a round into the chamber. Sunlight glinted off the barrel where the blueing had worn away.

Behind him, he heard the low chanting from the wounded Apache. A death song or a war song, he didn't know which.

Where was the other brave?

Hoofbeats throbbed in the silence.

Gunn reined up, listening. He turned his head, seeking out the direction of the sound.

From over a rise, three ponies galloped toward him. They were tightly packed together, nose to nose, and at first he thought they were riderless. On the left outside pony, though, a shape appeared—a painted face, hair flying, the snout of a rifle.

Gunn held his ground and brought the Winchester up to his shoulder.

He didn't aim at the man, but at the horse he clung to like a cow tick. He saw the rifle belch smoke, heard its crack a split second later, but he led the horse, chest high and squeezed the trigger.

The bullet from the Indian's rifle slashed over his head harmlessly, no more than a rush of air, a whisper of a death that might have been.

His own bullet caught the pony full in the chest. Its forelegs bent at the knees and the animal went down, tumbling. The other two ponies, lashed at the bridles, swung around, hit the ground and rolled, their legs flailing in the air. The Apache dove from his pony, as agile as a cat, and hit the ground running.

Gunn jacked another shell into the chamber.

The Apache ducked behind the fallen ponies. One was dead, the other two became tangled, struggling to sit upright, to rise.

Gunn heard the click as the Apache levered his rifle.

He looked for movement in back of the ponies. For a head, a hand, the rifle.

A deep silence hung on the air.

The ponies stopped struggling.

Esquire blew through his nostrils.

The chanting died away.

Gunn waited.

Sweat oiled his face, dripping salt into his eyes. He didn't blink, didn't move. The rifle was ready to throw down on his target. His breathing slowed, shallowed. Nothing moved. The sky was empty, the land desolate. Even the river seemed to have stopped.

Patience. The Apaches had more of it than any creature on earth. Gunn sat there under the blazing sun melting like candle wax. If he moved, he would expose himself for the briefest of moments. Even though he could not see his enemy, he felt that the Apache's eyes were on him. He could feel them boring into his own even though he could see nothing.

Was the Apache still behind the ponies?

Or had he moved, like a cloudshadow, over the sand only to rise up from another place as he had before.

There was no way of telling. It was as if the earth had swallowed the brave.

Yet, he was there.

Gunn could sense that he was still hidden behind the ponies. He itched to ride up and see for himself.

13

That, he knew, would likely prove fatal—for him.

That damned Apache patience. He could sit out here in the sun and bake like a lizard on a rock and the Apache wouldn't move. The sun sucked out all the moisture in his flesh. Sitting there, immobile, he became aware of how hot it was, how thirsty he was. His throat was parched, his lips were cracking from the torrid dryness. He could sit there and die in the saddle before the Apache would move. He had probably drunk so much water his tissues were soaked with it. That was the Apache way. A white man would sip at his water and die in the heat. The Indian drank it all until his belly was swollen and his bladder full and he could live two days in a desert that would kill a white man in twenty minutes.

Meanwhile, Gunn was a perfect target.

He sat there, sweat rippling from his armpits and soaking through his crotch, and wondered if he had a chance of smoking the Apache out. He could die out here in this hell. It was down to that. One on one. *Mano a mano.* He sat motionless, eyes narrowed, exploring the options. What would it take to make the Apache move first?

The rifle grew hot in his hands.

Gunn never twitched a muscle.

The seconds slogged by. The land buzzed with silence, somnolence.

The Apache could be circling him now, he thought. Sliding a fraction of an inch at a time, it might be done. With the right kind of patience.

He thought of a story he'd heard once on some trail, at some campfire. A man spoke of a tree full of turkey buzzards perched on the bare limbs of a tree. Nothing moved. Nothing was dead. Finally, one buzzard croaked to the others: "Patience, my ass, I'm going out

14

and kill something."

Patience.

The Apache had it. Gunn had only so much of it.

He was drowning in his own sweat.

His eyes stung with the constant drip of it. His armpits drained it down his sides. His hands were slick with it.

An idea struck him.

It might work.

It was better than waiting there like an iron stob, melting in the heat. It was better than waiting for a bullet that could come from any direction and blow his brains out.

"Fuck patience," he muttered.

Carefully, he wrapped the reins taut around the saddle horn.

Esquire fidgeted, shifted his weight, stood hipshot.

"Get on, boy!" he whispered, ramming his spurs up into the tender flanks. He felt them quiver as Esquire jumped, heading straight for the pile of Indian ponies.

Gunn slid out of the saddle and whopped his horse on the rump before he dropped to his knees.

Esquire galloped straight for the fallen ponies.

The Apache rose up from behind the dead one, leveling his rifle.

Gunn drew a bead and squeezed the trigger.

The bullet drove the brave backward four feet and slammed him into the ground, leaving a hole where his mouth had been. He made no sound. His rifle clattered on the stones as it fell from his grasp.

Gunn hobbled over and stared down at the mortally wounded Indian with cold gray eyes.

"Patience," he said quietly.

There was a rattling sound in the Apache's throat.

His eyes closed and his chest quivered, then stopped moving.

Smoke curled from the muzzle of Gunn's rifle. He drew a breath and turned away.

Quickly, he cut the two live ponies loose and shooed them away. He caught up with Esquire and reloaded the Winchester before shoving it back into his boot.

He rode for the river.

CHAPTER TWO

The Apache with the shattered shoulder crawled to the riverbank. He shoved a stick between his teeth and packed his wound with mud and moss. He passed out several times while he did this. He pulled on his bad arm and set the break. He passed out some more times. He repacked the wound. He untied his bandana, wrapped it around the wound, and drew it tight. He tied it using his teeth and one hand.

He stood up and staggered toward his pony. It eyed him warily, but the Indian made certain sounds that kept the pony's attention while he walked up to him. He climbed on its back, shuddering with pain.

He rode into the hills, his mind raging with hatred for one man.

The man with the blue steel eyes. The man with eyes like gun metal. The man who shot straight, who did not miss.

He knew where he had gone.

Toward Mesilla.

Where the old fort was, the fort they kept tearing down and moving and had finally left to the rats and lizards.

The Apache rode into the mountains where other

Mescaleros met him and heard his story.

Before nightfall, there was smoke in the sky.

There was smoke all along the trail, puffs rising from the hills at certain intervals.

The blankets smothered green wood and were taken away, so that the smoke rose in signaling clouds.

Sangre was alive.

His Mescaleros would paint their faces that night. That's what the smoke said, and more.

Sangre was the Apache with the broken shoulder.

His name, in Spanish, meant blood.

Gunn rested at the Cottonwoods. Six miles further on was Mesilla, a rich, fertile valley inhabited mostly by Mexicans. The stage station at the Cottonwoods had long since been abandoned, ever since the Butterfield Stage Line closed down in '61. The station was a crumbling mass of rafters and rotting adobe, infested with vermin. Gunn built a smoke, and watched the sun fall away in the sky. It was not yet cool, but he had swum in the river and his clothes were still damp. He looked at the far hills and saw the first puff of smoke.

Then another and another.

His eyes swept the cloudless horizon. Moments later, he saw another smoke puff. The cottony clouds seemed to float effortlessly up into the sky before an invisible high breeze blew them into lingering cobwebs.

A sudden chill gripped him.

More smoke appeared, miles away from atop a high butte out of range of his vision.

The cigarette tasted foul in his mouth.

He ground it out on his boot heel, went over to Esquire, and lifted up his left forefoot. He swore.

The horse could not be ridden another day without

being shod. The hoof was starting to splay out. As it was, the hoof would have to be trimmed considerably, pared down. He didn't want it splintering on the outsides. He checked the horse's hocks and fetlocks, all four legs. He rubbed each one firmly but tenderly. No, he had to find a blacksmith, maybe at one of the ranches. Or in Mesilla, although it was unlikely. Unless one of the Mexicans knew how to shoe a horse, he'd have to walk Esquire to the nearest rancho or hitch a ride on a freight wagon. Or buy a mule. Or—

There were no other options.

"I'm going to ride you a little ways, boy," said Gunn, patting Esquire's neck. "We'll take her easy."

Smoke signals dotted the sky as the sun sank over the western horizon. He didn't know what to make of them, except that something was brewing up in the hills. There was a lot of smoke and he had left one Apache alive. They had all been pretty determined to kill him. Yet he had done them no wrong. Six Apaches and they hadn't given up. That was mighty unusual. He thought, after the first two, that he had made his point. Now, it appeared, they had meant to keep him from reaching the river, or crossing it. Why? The only thing on the other side was an old stage road, an abandoned fort, and a valley full of Mexicans raising corn and chilis. It didn't make sense.

Unless there was something about to happen on the old stage road he didn't know about.

The road was full of shadows by the time Gunn reached Mesilla. The cool air drifted from the now-shallow river, meeting the warm air of the town and turning the atmosphere muggy. Esquire plodded at the slow pace Gunn had set, passing Mexicans who were still talking about the smoke in the sky. None of them seemed to know what it meant, but he detected the edge of fear in their voices.

He passed the irrigation ditches, smelled the fields with the summer crop not yet harvested. Dirty adobe shacks, shacks made of sticks and mud, lined the road. Children laughed and played, dogs barked. Deeper into the town, the houses got better, bigger, cleaner. People watched him pass and stayed to the shadows, their talk low, lazy. He heard them speak of the irrigation ditches drying up and of the beanstalks burning up in the fields. Indeed, the Rio Grande was mostly sand up this way, with barely a trickle of water since most of it had drained off into the ditches.

At the center of the village, he came to the plaza. The cantinas glowed with lamplight that spilled out onto the street. The small Mesilla Hotel was the tallest adobe there. Horses stood hipshot at the hitch rails in front of the hotel and adjoining cantina. Talk drifted Gunn's way and he realized that it was coming from the cantina.

He rode up and dismounted. He tried to read the brands on the horses. A man could learn a lot from the way a man's saddle was rigged, or the mark on a horse's hip. There were three horses there, solid animals with good legs. They had California saddles and rifles. The horses were not warm, so the men who rode them must be leaving, not arriving. That, in itself, was curious. Ranchers, he thought, who had spent a day in town, were having a last drink before heading home.

The town smelled of drying chilis and onions, tobacco and beans, corn flour and *salsa casera*. He was hungry and his stomach churned when he caught the aroma of *tortillas* and *frijoles*.

The name outside of the cantina was blurred by weather and the dim light from the lamps inside. He stepped into the cantina.

Mexicans hunched over tables. A rotund lady in a colorful dress carried steaming plates to a corner table occupied by swarthy men in white shirts and trousers, sombreros hanging like tortoise shells on their backs. Three men stood at the far end of the bar, watching him as he blinked in the sudden light and took his bearings.

One of the men who looked at him was a breed. Half-Apache, from the looks of him. The other two were white, one of them vaguely familiar. In any other place, they'd be classed as hard cases. Here, any man living on the rough edge of civilization had to be hard. Gunn saw the look in their eyes as he stepped up to the bar. These were men used to having their own way, able to walk a wide path with no one getting in their way. The Mexicans avoided them, deferred to them with politeness and wariness and fear. The men wore pistols and knives and they did not have the look of ranchers about to head home after a drink.

Rather, they seemed on edge, nervous about his being there. Their problem. He had no quarrel with them, no business with them.

The bartender hesitated, looked at one of the men at the end of the bar who nodded almost imperceptibly. Gunn wondered about that. But the bartender came over, waddling like a fat goose. He was fat and dark, with leathery skin crinkled at the eyes, and swatches of crimson on his cheeks where the blood stayed close to the surface. He had thick eyebrows, a moustache, long sideburns, and long straight black hair.

"*Si, señor?*"

"Whiskey," said Gunn.

"*No hay.*"

"*Pues,* tequila."

"*A sus ordenes,*" he said, most politely. Too politely.

The man brought a bottle of tequila and a shot glass. He poured it full and left the bottle.

21

"Beintecinco centavos oro," said the bartender quickly. Gunn threw a silver dollar on the bar. The price was twenty-five cents, not in gold as the dialect would indicate, but in American coin, rather than Mexican *plata,* silver. The bartender did not pick up the dollar, but left it there in case Gunn wanted another drink. He had listened carefully to the sound of the dollar hitting the wood bar. He wouldn't have to bite it to see if it was genuine.

"Do you speak English?" Gunn asked him.

"Jess, I speak *Ingles.*"

"Need a horse shod. You got a blacksmith in town?"

The Mexican shrugged.

The men at the end of the bar laughed.

"Something funny?" Gunn asked, lifting his glass.

"Where the hell you think you are, stranger? El Paso?"

The man who spoke had a thick face in the shape of a spade, thick neck, muscular shoulders. He stood about five foot six or seven, seemed solid, that part of him Gunn could see above the bar. His hat was pushed back away from his forehead. He looked about thirty, rough as a cob. The other man, the one he thought he had seen before, was slightly taller, with a sun-darkened face lumpy from some kind of childhood disease. He had hazel eyes, a thin moustache, and flared sideburns like a gambler's or a drummer's. He and the breed said nothing. Their expressions were impassive.

"Are you saying there's no blacksmith in Mesilla?" said Gunn evenly.

The three men laughed again. This time, Gunn looked at the man in the middle. He knew who he was. The mention of El Paso helped.

Abe Jennings. Oh, he'd changed some, but it was the same man.

The eyes were the same, the moustache and

sideburns were new. The lumps on his face that looked like hornet stings had once been covered with a beard. The man was older, heavier. Ten years, twelve maybe, since Gunn had seen him. He had worked as a rawhider, then a stage driver for the Butterfield stage outfit. He had worked six months, and then had been fired for robbing a wealthy passenger. A man found some things hard to live down. Gunn had run across him in Mexico and El Paso, heard of him with one deal and another. It was said he had killed a couple of men, but never spent a day in jail. Mostly, they ran him off and he turned up somewhere else. There were such men in the West and no one ever seemed to put much effort into using the law to stop them. The men Jennings was said to have killed were no accounts—no families, no one to protest their deaths. And, maybe they were at fault, too. No one gave a damn. Jennings never stayed in one place long enough to pin down. When there was trouble, people noticed him, and by that time, he was gone.

"There ain't no smithy in Mesilla," said Jennings. "You'd best ride on, friend."

Gunn considered the offer.

"Are you speaking for the town or for yourself, mister?"

Jennings frowned.

"I'm speaking for you, friend. The Messicans here don't have no horses and no iron shoes. You got to go to El Paso for all that."

"Maybe I'll have to buy a mule. My horse can't be rode without shoes."

"The Injuns been ridin' horses for years thouten iron shoes," said the man next to Jennings. "I don't hear them complainin'."

Gunn tossed off the rest of his tequila, then poured another shot. Some of the Mexicans, sensing the

23

tension in the room, got up and left. The bartender busied himself underneath the bar. Gunn watched him out of the corner of his eye. He didn't want him coming up with something dangerous in his hands.

Inside the space of a few moments, the room emptied. There were only the three men at the end of the bar, the bartender down on his hands and knees, and Gunn.

"Well, now," said Jennings, "look what you gone and done. People just don't like strangers here. Unless they're crop buyers or farmers. You don't look like either to me, stranger."

Gunn leveled his gaze at Jennings. He shifted his weight. His right hand dropped to his side, out of sight of the three men. He lifted his drink with his left hand.

The three men got the message.

"I've been places," said Gunn, "where I had to drink with my pistol on the bar it was so crowded. I can do the same here."

Jennings started to say something, then backed off. A look came over his face. A look of recognition.

The man next to him opened his mouth to say something. His right hand jerked away from his whiskey glass. Jennings put an arm on his hand as it started to slide off the bar.

"Hold it, Kelly," said Jennings. "I seen that man before. Ain't I friend? Down to El Paso, some spell back. Or Houston. You a cowman?"

"Was," admitted Gunn.

Jennings seemed to be wrestling with the identification of the stranger. Kelly continued to glare at Gunn. The breed's face froze to a noncommittal mask. The bartender looked up as if to see for himself why it had suddenly gotten so quiet. He squatted beneath the bar, busy with something underneath.

Seconds ticked by, with Jennings squinting, thinking. Suddenly, he lifted his hand away from Kelly's and snapped his fingers.

"You was at Luna Creek. Palomas. All of them widows. You drove cattle from El Paso out there and— Jesus, you're Gunn."

Gunn nodded.

"Gunn?" said Kelly.

The breed's expression changed. His face seemed to darken.

"Cartucho," he said.

Kelly's face drained of color.

"You *that* Gunn?" he asked. "The one what was up in the Brazos Valley, run Cartucho down?"

"He's the one," said Jennings.

Gunn said nothing.

The breed looked uncomfortable. The bartender looked up at Gunn. The color in his cheeks had disappeared. His lips were quivering. He stood up and moved slowly down the bar toward Jennings.

"Mister," said Kelly, "you done cut a wide swath here and there. They still talk of you over to Palomas and there ain't an Apache in New Mexico Territory don't know your name."

"Buy you a drink," said Jennings, his voice laden with a mollifying tone.

"My drink's paid for," said Gunn. His right hand still hovered near the butt of his Colt. "And I'm still looking for a blacksmith."

Jennings started to say something, but before he could speak they heard the sound of a wagon rumbling into the square, and the beat of horses' hooves. Voices drifted into the cantina. The wagon or whatever it was stopped just outside. Traces rattled, wheels groaned, springs creaked.

The three men looked up, then looked at each other. Before Gunn knew what was happening, they headed

25

for the kitchen door, leaving their drinks. One minute they were there, the next, they were gone. The door closed behind them and the bartender stood frozen, looking at Gunn with watery eyes. Another door, beyond the kitchen, slammed shut. Voices in the kitchen rose up, died.

"Mighty spooky, ain't they?" said Gunn.

"I don't know, *señor*. They leave quick."

Gunn turned as a man entered the cantina. He was covered with dust, and wore a wide-brimmed hat that was cracked at the brim, swept back. A huge kerchief ringed his neck. His shirt was wet with sweat, stained at the armpits. His face was moon shaped and bearded. The beard was roan, once red, now turning the color of white clay. He wore a pistol.

"Jorge," he barked, "that *cocinera,* she still back there in the kitchen? I got passengers and they're hungry as cats. And I'm thirsty as a poisoned he-wolf."

"*Si,* Mulejaw," said Jorge. "Maria's here. She will cook."

"I got four *pasajeros* and three of 'em's wimmin, so get out your tablecloth and set 'em a table. I'll have some of your mezcal."

Mulejaw, Gunn thought, looked as tough as an oak stump. He had heard of him, knew him to be one hell of a jehu.

"You bringing a stage through?" Gunn asked. "Thought you was a freighter."

"I am, mister, and I got troubles. Freight wagon's on its way with a busted axle all roped up. Hit a sump hole in the Coloraddy and like to broke my wagon in half. Too damned heavy for one thing. Do I know you?"

"The name's Gunn."

"Ned Wales," said the man, barreling toward Gunn. "They call me 'Mulejaw.'"

Gunn held out his hand, but he froze when he saw

26

two women come through the doorway and stand there like statues.

They were young, and they were as pretty as anything he had ever seen. Beautiful, even.

And, as sure as they were there, he knew it was the wrong place for them to be.

Even as Mulejaw was shaking his hand as if to jerk it out of its wrist socket, he knew he was looking pure trouble square in the face.

CHAPTER THREE

The two young ladies stared at Gunn. They saw a tall, over-six-foot man with wide lean shoulders, light brown hair, gray eyes, and sensuous lips. They giggled and looked at one another. Their traveling dresses failed to conceal hourglass figures.

"Who's your friend, Mr. Wales?" said one.

An older woman wearing horn-rimmed spectacles primly walked through the door. She wore her light brown hair swept back in a bun. Her bonnet threw her face in shadow, but she had sharp features, a long thin nose, high cheekbones, and an oddly sensuous mouth. She wore no makeup and her slenderness was accented by her height. She was at least five foot seven, Gunn judged, in her stocking feet.

"Never mind, Miss Longworth," she snapped. "We don't talk to strangers. Amity, you and Janice find a table and seat yourselves."

Mulejaw grinned as he released Gunn's hand. Gunn felt the numbness go away. The women glided toward a table. The cook, Maria, came out of the kitchen and spoke politely to the ladies.

"Them's some of my passengers," said Wales, as Jorge brought him a bottle of mezcal and a glass. "A couple more comin' on the freight wagon. Mezcal?"

"I'll stay with the tequila," said Gunn. "I'd like to ride with you to the Gila. My horse needs shoeing and he won't make the ride with me on him."

"Cost you forty dollars. High, I reckon, but take it or leave it. Those folks done hired the coach all the way to San Bernardino."

"Done. But what are ladies doing riding a stage? The U.P. not running anymore?"

"The ladies come from schools back east, through Kansas, spent some time in Dallas, visitin', and then more of the same in El Paso. You can find out all about 'em if you ride with us."

"I'm hungry myself," said Gunn.

"We're staying the night next door at the hotel. You're welcome to break bread with us."

"Obliged."

"Set that table for five," said Mulejaw to Maria. "And another table for the men due in the next hour."

Maria nodded. She billowed a checkered tablecloth in front of the three ladies who sat stiffly in their chairs. The young women seemed excited to be in such a place, but the matron with them sniffed the air with wary condescension.

Wales poured himself a drink and leaned over the bar. He spoke to Gunn in low tones that did not carry beyond them.

"Don't want to alarm the ladies, but I saw smoke this afternoon. Up in the hills."

"Yes. I saw it too. Something's up."

"Damned niggardly Apaches. Stirred up for some damned reason. You good with that Colt pistol?"

"I've used it."

"Freight might be temptin' to a Injun."

"How so?"

"Rifles," said Mulejaw. "Spencer repeaters. Now,

29

wouldn't that be sweet to see a bunch of painted Mescaleros getting their hands on a case or two of Spencers?"

Gunn's eyes narrowed to slits.

He didn't want to think about it.

Hortense Bangs was not as old as she looked from a distance. Gunn judged her to be in her late twenties, perhaps a shade over thirty. He learned that she was a spinster; she had never been West before, nor out of Boston. Her charges, Janice Longworth and Amity Heller, however, were from Sacramento and Monterey, respectively.

Janice was eighteen, blond, blue eyed, with apple cheeks, a pert, upturned nose, and dimples when she smiled, which was often. She was both impetuous and impulsive, fawning over Gunn to Miss Bangs's constant irritation. Over steaks and beans, *tortillas* and *salsa casera,* Janice kept up a constant chatter, proclaiming her interest in horses and men, as well as outlining her goal to raise a family and horses on her father's Sacramento rancho.

Amity Heller, by contrast, was dark haired and brown eyed, smoldering with a voluptuousness that belied her nineteen years. Gunn learned that she was the daughter of an Army prig, a widower. According to Amity, he felt he had to assume her proper social place as his housekeeper, hostess, and dance partner since her mother's death three years before. Amity did not seem to relish her position in furthering her father's career and treated Miss Bangs as the enemy, as a cohort in her father's campaign to make her into something she wasn't. She loved the Monterey coast and the Spanish peoples there, the hills, the thick woods, and open spaces. She loved the beans and *tortillas* and sprinkled generous doses of hot sauce on her beef.

Ned Wales listened to the chatter and ate like a starving wolf, helped by generous swallows of warm beer. Every time he spoke to Hortense Bangs, the latter reeled back in her chair, obviously distraught at the odor of his breath. She merely picked at her food and kept fixing Gunn with a baleful, accusing eye, as if he had already bedded her wards in his mind. Indeed, Janice made no effort to hide her interest in the pale-eyed man, while Amity was more reserved, sending coy glances Gunn's way only when she thought no one else was looking.

Gunn felt uncomfortable. He spoke little of himself, despite Miss Bangs's critical, injudicious probing.

"You're a single man, Mr. Gunn?"

"There's no mister attached, Miss Bangs. Just Gunn. I'm a widower."

"I see."

"How does a handsome man like you avoid being married?" asked Janice Longworth.

"Thank you for the compliment, Miss," said Gunn, "and I can't answer that."

Laughter from Janice, a frown from Hortense. Amity scanned his face with bright dark eyes.

Ned Wales belched loudly to Miss Bangs's discomfort and dismay.

He patted his belly, oblivious to Hortense's disapproving stare.

"Talk to you a minute, Gunn," he said. "When you're finished foofarawing the ladies."

"I'll have a smoke outside with you, Wales," said Gunn. He picked up his hat from the floor and slid away from the table. "Ladies, thank you for the conversation and the company."

"Are you staying at the hotel, Mr. Gunn?" drilled Hortense.

"I reckon. If they have a bed for me."

"Fine. Be sure you keep your door securely locked. I wouldn't want your sleep disturbed."

"I sleep right sound, Miss Bangs. Being alone, I don't have to worry about someone snoring or poking me in the ribs during the night."

Wales laughed at the exchange. Miss Bangs huffed and the girls smiled at him as he bowed his leave. He noticed that Miss Bangs had clear hazel eyes flecked with green and gold. Her glasses magnified them. Her unpainted lips pursed as if she had to struggle to keep from delivering a retort.

"Naughty girls," he heard Miss Bangs say as he walked outside with Ned Wales. "Shame, shame."

"Walk with me to the livery," said Wales, outside. "You'll want to put up your horse."

"They have a livery but no blacksmith?"

"An empty adobe. Boy feeds and watches the horses for a dollar or two."

Gunn helped Wales unhitch his team. He followed, leading Esquire, as Wales led the four horses past the statue in the center of the plaza and down a street. A large low adobe with a wooden gate on it served as the stables. There were stalls separated by poles inside. A couple of young Mexicans rose up out of a pile of straw to help get the horses out of their bridles. Gunn unsaddled Esquire.

"Best take your gear with you," said Wales.

Gunn lugged his saddle, blanket, bedroll, Winchester, scabbard, and saddlebags outside. It was a clear, starry night. The moon had not yet risen, but its glow silvered the sky over the hills in the distance. Wales stopped, fishing for a smoke in his pockets. Gunn lay his saddle over a hitch rail and piled the gear on top. He built a smoke, struck a match, and lit both their cigarettes.

"Knowed who you was when I seed you," said Wales.

"Huh?"

"Kiddin' you 'bout that Colt on your hip. Minute I heard the name, the bell rung. Folks're still talkin' 'bout that business over to Palomas. You and your partner, what's his name?"

"Randall. Jed Randall."

"What ever happened to him?"

"He's dead. Killed."

"Sorry to hear it."

"He was a man to ride the river with." Gunn's cigarette glowed in the dark. Inside the livery, the horses settled down and crunched on grain. The Mexican boys chattered musically, their voices muffled. Up the street, a dog barked. Someone plucked a guitar, and its disembodied notes floated to their ears.

"We got a situation here, Gunn. Can I trust you?"

"Depends."

"That freight wagon. Might be somethin' the Apaches're interested in. What it's carryin'."

"None of my business."

Wales heaved a sigh. He rested an arm on the hitch rail, and looked up at Gunn's shadowy face.

"That's good enough for me. Feller named Jacob Hallman's carrying those Spencer repeaters to a special cavalry outfit quartered up on the Gila. Apache hunters. You ever hear of a buck named Sangre?"

"No."

"Mean. Mescalero. Cavalry trained at Fort Yuma special for this one. But they need those new Spencers and Hallman's bringin' them out. That smoke today means Sangre knows about 'em and we think we know how he come by that information."

Gunn felt something cold crawling up his spine. The

33

horses that had been tied in front of the cantina hadn't been there when he and Ed had left. It was a good bet that the owners were riding somewhere. They hadn't wanted to see Wales. Or, rather, they hadn't wanted Wales to see them.

"Go on," said Gunn.

"There was some trouble a couple of weeks ago in El Paso. Mexican worked for me in the freight office. Name of Ben Aguilar. He knew about Hallman and the Spencers. The army picked my line as the best one to get through with those rifles. It was supposed to be a secret. Ben handled all the paper work. One night he was jumped and taken to a room. He was tortured for a goddamned week. They burnt him with cigarettes, used a knife on him, cut off some fingers. Finally, he told them what they wanted to know. He showed up a week ago looking like bloody hell. Died two days ago. He had to write everything out for us. But we got the names."

"He couldn't talk?"

"They didn't cut all of his fingers off. Left a couple. Burned out his eyes. The last thing they did after he talked was to cut out his tongue."

Gunn sucked in a breath.

"The names, Wales—"

"Abe Jennings was the main one. His partners were Mick Kelly, a damned owlhooter, and a half-breed Apache name of Choya. This Choya's a snake and his mother is Sangre's sister."

"Wished I had run into you two days ago," said Gunn. "Or even yesterday."

"How come?"

Gunn told him about the six Apaches, about the one he left alive. He told him about running into Jennings, Kelly, and the breed, earlier that evening.

Wales whistled and tossed his cigarette away, leaving

34

a flurry of orange sparks in its wake.

"You get a good look at the brave you shot in the shoulder?"

"He was about twenty-five, short, flat nose, black and white paint—black forehead, white streaks across his nose, on his cheeks, black chin."

"Jesus H. Christ! That was Sangre hisself. Boy, you got yourself an enemy for damned sure. And Jennings is probably a-settin' in his camp right now tellin' him I come in to Mesilla."

Gunn knew that Wales was probably right.

"He probably searched the coach before he left," said Gunn. "Looking for those rifles."

"That's why we run the wagon separate. Even Ben Aguilar didn't know we was goin' to do that. But, now we got to do some reloading. The wagon won't make it and those rifles got to get through. We get to Tucson I got to tell Clarita and her brother, Felix about Ben. It'll make 'em both sick."

"Ben was their father?"

"Brother."

Gunn ground his cigarette out on his boot heel and hefted his saddle and gear. The two walked back to the cantina.

"Why is Jennings hooked up with Sangre?" he asked Wales.

"Man is plumb loco. Carried a grudge against Butterfield for gettin' fired, hell, ten, twelve years ago. Then he got hot at others who run the lines and wouldn't hire him. Oh, some did, but he didn't last long. I wouldn't hire him and he threatened me. Paid no attention to it. Then he took up with this Choya and Kelly. Kelly's crazy as he is. Got a tin plate in his head. Heard he shot a man once't just for snorin' in his sleep."

"Nice bunch," said Gunn.

"Real sweet. Speakin' of that, you already met the

womenfolks. I'd stay clear of those two schoolgirls if was I you. They're man hungry and Miss Bangs watches 'em like a hawk. I'll bet she'd eat a man alive was he to try and spark one of her precious little chickens."

Gunn laughed.

"Mulejaw, you're talking to a saint."

Wales laughed and slapped his thigh.

"We'll see what a saint you are, a-settin' in that coach with those two gals."

"I think I'll ride on top."

"Good. Besides Hallman, we got a young buck with us ain't dry behind the ears. Name of Yancy. Meredith Yancy. He's got too much money and he's just inherited some more. But he wants to be a Westerner. He's twenty-five years old and a bit of a dandy, but he'll be all right once that bone in his head gets transferred to his back."

"Sounds like a fun trip," said Gunn wryly.

"Mister, you don't know what fun is. Hallman will back you. He's got a good head, can shoot like Dan'l Boone. He's ex-army and they don't come any straighter."

At the hotel, Gunn found a room, while Wales tended to the luggage on the stage. The room was clean, Spartan: a big bed, table, chairs, a dresser, small tin mirror, water bowl and pitcher, two old lamps that smoked, and some religious pictures on the adobe walls. It was low ceilinged, and he had to hunch over to walk around. He turned in after washing some of the dust off his face.

Later, around midnight, a knock on the door awakened him.

Groggily, he shook off sleep.

"Yeah?"

"It's me," said a whispering female voice.

Gunn's first thought was that one of the young ladies had come to his room.

"Go away," he said.

"Mr. Gunn, please—"

He was wrong.

Hortense Bangs was at his door.

CHAPTER FOUR

Gunn lighted a lamp and opened the door.

Hortense furtively looked both ways down the hall, then came into the room. She wore a light pink wrap over her nightgown. The nightgown rustled when she walked.

"Lock the door," she said.

Gunn turned the key. He rubbed sleep from his eyes. He had on only a pair of trousers. He padded barefoot over to the bed and sat down. Hortense stood by the table like a statue. Her glasses shimmered with the coppery light from the lamp. Smoke crawled up the wall, leaving a black trail on the whitewashed clay.

"Some reason you wake a man up in the middle of the night? Your ladies aren't here, Miss Bangs. They haven't been here and I haven't been to their rooms, either."

"I know," she said, fluffing her chignon. She didn't sit down, but stood there, looking at his bare chest, his shoulders. She drew in a breath, and held it. In the light, she was not unattractive. Without the bulky dress, her lean figure was not so spare. She had curves. Her breasts were hidden melons under the silky robe, full rounded, symmetrical. House slippers peeked from beneath her nightgown. "I—I waited until I was sure they were asleep before I came to your room."

"You're all in the same room?"

"Yes."

"You don't take any chances, do you?"

"I am responsible for them, Mr. Gunn."

"And what about yourself?"

"I am responsible for my own actions."

Gunn shook his head and sighed.

"In some quarters, maybe in Boston, it's not considered proper for a woman to come to a man's hotel room at night, unless there's a fire or some other emergency."

"May I sit down?" she said, her voice quavering.

"Yes, ma'am." He wondered when she was going to come to the point. He had entertained women in his rooms before, but Miss Bangs was not one he would have figured to knock on his door. She obviously had something on her mind, but she seemed to be in no hurry to tell him what it was. Sometimes, he thought, women could be aggravating, but this one was harder to figure out than most.

"I know I'm behaving badly," she said, a husk to her voice that he had not noticed before. "I'm well aware that according to Boston standards, perhaps to yours as well, my coming here does not seem proper. Please don't interrupt me, Mr. Gunn. I'm determined to say what is on my mind.

"When I was given the opportunity to come West, supervising these two young ladies, I welcomed the chance to leave a rather stifling existence. I have been a schoolteacher ever since I was a very young lady. My parents were quite strict and I was subjected to a rigid conformity in our straight-laced community. Yet I always yearned for adventure, for unknown places. Like many other young ladies of my generation, however, I lacked both opportunity and courage to act out my private wishes.

"Now, I find that I relish the newfound freedom this trip has given me. I have met a lot of interesting people on this journey. You, however, are the most interesting of all."

Gunn waited for her to go on, but she sat there, primly regarding him, waiting for him to respond to her little speech.

"You talk a lot," he said, "but don't say much. We have a long ride together. You could have told me all this tomorrow."

She drew herself up and folded her hands in her lap.

"No," she said, "I couldn't. I thought I could be frank with you. I also came close to making a fool of myself with Mr. Hallman."

"Hallman?"

"Yes. He will be riding with us tomorrow, I'm told by Mr. Wales. I am a spinster, Mr. Gunn. Not by choice, but by circumstances. I have lived a cloistered life, shut away from the normal commerce between males and females. I worked for a girls' school and seldom had the opportunity to engage in conversation with the opposite sex. Do you comprehend the temper of what I am trying to convey to you?"

Gunn's mouth hung open like a gopher hole.

"Lady," he said, "I don't savvy but about every fifth word. You're way over my head."

"Oh I doubt that, Mr. Gunn."

"Well, we just don't talk that way out here. Life is short and most of us try to get to the point real quick."

"Yes. I see. The point is, sir, that I wish—I want— you to take me to bed. I'm not a virgin, but I'm relatively inexperienced. I—I'm just—well, I'd be glad to make it worth your while. I have funds in my room and tomorrow, I'll be glad to meet your price—"

40

Gunn's jaw dropped. Suddenly he understood what Miss Bangs was saying. His heart wrenched in his chest as if someone had squeezed it with a velvet glove. He looked closely at the woman and saw that she was embarrassed, ashamed, and deadly serious.

"Miss Bangs," he said slowly, "have you been drinking?"

"A—a little."

"Look, ma'am, you don't have to lay yourself out like this for a man. You're an uncommon woman, and a lot of men would probably want to spark you if you came off your high horse. I think you just need rest and some time to think. A trip like this, in a hot dusty stage, can scramble your brains."

"Please," she said, "don't turn me down like Hallman. I—I couldn't take that."

"Hallman? You asked him to—"

"Well, not in so many words. I, ah, approached him in El Paso, let him know my room number and I waited for him. I waited and waited and he never came—"

She began crying then and Gunn felt as if his heart had been jerked out of his chest. Her sobs boomed in the room.

He got up from the bed and went to her. He took her head in his hands and held it up so he could look into her eyes. Her glasses were smeared with tears.

"Don't, ma'am. You make it awful hard on a man."

"I—I can't help it," she stammered. "No man wants me. I'm just an old spinster."

"No you're not. You're pretty and a lot of men would—"

"They wouldn't! They haven't! Oh, Mr. Gunn, I'm so ashamed. I saw you tonight, the way those girls looked at you and I knew what they were feeling, because I wanted to flirt with you too. I wanted you to look at me and put your hand on me and hold me and kiss me—

my heart fluttered and you looked right past me, like all the rest. Yes, I had some liquor. A little wine for courage. I tried to get you out of my mind and tried to stop from making a fool of myself, but—I just felt hot all over and restless and so empty I wanted to die."

She closed her eyes and jerked her head out of his hands. He stood there, helpless, not knowing what to do.

Rising to her feet, she stood there, trembling.

"I—I'll be all right in a moment. Give me a minute."

"Miss Bangs, you can't torture yourself like this. I— I—well, I mean, I think I know how you feel. When you want someone real bad, but they don't want you—it's hell. It tears you up inside."

"Do you know, Mr. Gunn? Do you really know?"

"I know what it's like to want something you can't have."

She tried to stop crying, her whimpers shaking her body as she tried to stem the tide of tears. He put his hands on her shoulders and shook her gently.

"Don't cry, ma'am."

She sniffled and took a deep breath.

Her eyes locked on his. She smelled of lilac water and silk, a strange mingling of female musk and bath soap that clogged his nostrils, made him giddy at the closeness of her. Her hazel eyes seemed possessed of latent secrets, sparkling with a yearning that he understood—a loneliness he had often felt himself since the death of his wife, Laurie. Tradition, moral standards, a certain code of his day told him that Hortense Bangs had no business being there in his room. But an animal sense of his own nature and of a woman's own desires belied all such mores. What he had been taught was not so. Woman needed man and man needed woman. They came together, natural, if possible, and something inside each of them canceled

42

out all laws and customs. Flesh went after flesh and the Bible was only a black book on a table or a pulpit, something someone wrote a long time ago when lust was not concealed by long dresses and high collars.

Hortense Bangs exuded an animal sensuality that tugged at his loins, drew him to her. Her silken robe was soft to the touch. Her eyes begged him, the light in them gaunt and raw as passion itself.

"Damn," he muttered to himself. But their eyes were locked and he felt her drawing close to him. Her hands, soft as bird wings, sought his waist, touched him, slid around to his back.

"Yes," she said, "you feel as good as I thought you would."

He wanted to say no, to push her away. He felt the pressure of her fingers on his back, pulling him close to her. He felt himself drowning in her womanly scent. He wanted to hide from the frankness of her gaze, the awful yearning he saw in her eyes. He wanted to run from the challenge of her unseen body; he could sense its pulse as she drew him near. She was not so much bold as desperate, not so much wanton as hungry as a tame cat is hungry to be petted, to be stroked, to be chucked under the chin.

Hortense Bangs was a firelight and a candle glowing in a window. She was a song played on a lonesome guitar, the words of a poem read late at night when the world is quiet, the land asleep. She was something purring next to his ear, something brushing furry against his leg. She was someone who broke with upbringing and the traditional rules for proper female behavior. She was someone who smiled at him now, faintly, with a pleading in her eyes that melted his own iron code into something malleable, like clay.

He tilted her chin up, and kissed her smoldering lips. A fire shot through him as she tightened her embrace.

She drew his loins into hers, into the soft concavity of her thighs. He lingered on her lips, drawing sweetness out of her mouth, tasting the wetness, the warmth.

"What's happening?" she husked, when he broke the kiss.

"I don't know."

"I can feel you."

He was hard.

"Yes," he said.

"Did I do that?"

"Yes."

She reached down, touching the bulge in his trousers.

"It's true," she said. "It's really true."

He could not tell her why he wanted her now. He didn't know. He put his hands around her waist and drew her close. The hardness grew, and touched her softness. She offered her lips to him. He bent, kissing her again. A surge of heat rippled through him.

Her hand squeezed his manhood. He felt his knees go weak. Her touch was delicate, yet, she had him in her grip. He drove a tongue inside her mouth as if to violate her straight-laced ethics, but she surprised him again. Her tongue turned into a coiling, stabbing creature, prying his own lips apart, tangling with his own probing tongue.

Breathless, she looked up at him in wonder.

"You're doing things to me," she said.

"And you to me."

"You won't—won't hurt me, will you, Gunn?"

"Hurt you?"

"Leave me—unsatisfied. Unfulfilled. I—I couldn't stand that. Not after coming this far."

"I want you, Miss Bangs."

"Hortense."

"I want you, woman."

44

She shivered all over, and stepped away from him.

He stood there dumbly as she took off her glasses and lay them on the table. She reached up with her hands, and began undoing the chignon. Hair cascaded down her back. She shook it out. Lamplight played on the light strands, highlighting the sheen of her tresses.

"I want you too," she said. "I think I've wanted you all my life."

Gunn cursed softly. With her hair down, the glasses off, she looked beautiful. Radiant. As he watched, dumbstruck, she slipped off her robe. Her breasts peeked from behind the satiny lace of her nightgown. The nightgown clung to her body, hugged the curves with a shining grace. She slipped the straps from her shoulders and the gown fell in a puddle at her feet. She stood there, her arms drawn up over her breasts, shyly waiting for him to come to her, to take her to his bed.

"God, you're beautiful," he husked.

"Am I?"

"Yes. Where have you been hiding? Why?"

"Oh, Gunn, don't tease me, please."

"You're a wonder, Hortense. A blooming wonder."

He doffed his trousers, and came to her naked. His manhood jutted out from his loins, a sleek throbbing creature pulsing with engorged blood. She stared at it, taking it in her hand as he drew close. She squeezed and closed her eyes as a shudder, like a current of electricity, passed through her.

He saw her breasts in full view for the first time. The nipples taut nubbins rising out of dark aureoles like elfin faces, the mounds full and creamy soft like honeydew melons. She was lean and yet oddly voluptuous, trim as a thoroughbred, with finely turned ankles, slender legs, and gracefully curved hips.

He kissed her savagely, overcome by a sudden lust. Yet he was not brutal, but only full of a raging hunger.

His manhood throbbed in her hand. His pulse hammered in his temples as she returned his kiss, her mouth wet and steamy, tasting faintly of wine and crushed mint.

He carried her to the bed. She was light in his arms, curled there, staring up at him like a trusting child. Her eyes glistened with a thin film of moisture, the gold and the green dazzling as precious gems. He lay her down in the center of the bed and crawled in beside her.

When he touched her, she trembled.

He kissed her mouth, touched her between her legs. He stroked the tender mound, the labials of her sex, the fine light hairs of her pubic thatch. He kissed her behind the ears, on the neck and the chest. He took a nipple into his mouth, tongued it until it thickened like a thumb. She quivered, and cooing sounds came from her mouth. He felt her legs and thighs, and roamed over her slender body with exploring fingers. He took the other breast in his mouth, suckled at it until she quivered all over.

"Gunn—" she breathed.

Her voice sounded far away, muffled.

"Yes?"

"I—I don't know what to say—I'm confused—this, this isn't the way it's supposed to be. You're not what I—what I expected."

"How is it supposed to be?"

"My mother—she told me that men were brutal, that lust was a sin. She said that men didn't care about women. That a man was just—just an animal. She said it would be horrible."

"What would be horrible?"

"This. You."

"Why? How did she know this?"

"I guess—my father. She hated to—to do things with him. I was her only child."

46

"But you said I was not the first, Hortense. You sound as though you don't really know. You sound like a virgin."

She sighed.

"No, I'm not a virgin. But I'm not exactly experienced. I was—was about the same age as Janice or Amity when it happened. And it wasn't love. My—my uncle, he came into my room and he put his thing inside me. He didn't say anything. It hurt a little and then he was ashamed and started crying and begged me not to say anything. I never did. He never touched me again. No man has."

"Good Lord," said Gunn.

"You're tender and considerate. I—I just don't know what to think. I feel cheated. Lied to."

"Maybe you were," he said, crawling over her. He held her in his arms, and gently pried her legs apart with his knee. "I want you, Hortense. Just relax. I'll go slow. There's plenty of time."

"Yes, slow. I'd like that. I'm a little frightened, but I trust you."

He slid into her then and she screamed. Not in pain, but in ecstasy. Her fingernails dug into his shoulders as her body shook. He held on to her as the climax jolted her senses, shaking her body with electric fingers.

She was wet and hot, smooth as oiled fur inside. He slid in slowly, letting her grow used to him. She stared up at him with wide eyes and he smiled. He slid deeper and her mouth opened. Deeper and her lips quivered.

"Yes," she breathed. "Now I know."

"What do you know?"

"That you are not like other men. You look mean and hard, but you're gentle. A gentle man. I envy her. She must have been special."

"Who?"

"Your wife."

"Hush, woman. You want to know everything all at once. Be yourself. Forget what your mother told you, forget your father, your uncle. This is you and your life, your body. It doesn't belong to anyone else. It doesn't even belong to me."

She closed her eyes then and he saw tears squeeze out through the lids and stream down her cheeks.

He stroked her slowly, sliding his swollen organ in and out of her steam-wet tunnel. She bucked with repeated orgasms, shaking her head, crying out at her mother, at the lies she had been told. Gunn lanced her until she thrashed out of control, until their bodies were sleek with sweat. Until he could stand it no longer.

She embraced him as he shot his seed like a bolt from a crossbow.

The lamp wick burned low, and black smoke spread like a shadow across the wall. The room danced as the flame wavered.

"Gunn," she said later, "I can't thank you. There aren't words."

"I'm the one who owes thanks. You came here. I'm mighty grateful. You're an uncommon woman, Hortense."

"And you're an uncommon man, Gunn. I know that. My mother wasn't completely wrong."

"No, not completely."

"We almost missed each other, didn't we, Gunn?"

The wick fluttered and the lamp went out. The room sank into darkness. Hortense reached out for him in the dark and touched his chest. Her fingers traced a path up his jawline, over his eyes. He wanted her again.

And yes, she was right. They had almost missed each other, and life would have been less rich had she not come to him, had he not known her as a man is meant to know a woman.

CHAPTER FIVE

Jacob Hallman pulled his ailing wagon into Mesilla at dawn. The regular driver was not on the seat and Hallman didn't mind that. He was weary from wrestling with mechanical things, and bone sore, blistered from the sun, and annoyed at delays. He was also concerned over the smoke signals he had seen in the sky the day before when he and the other two men had waded, crippled, across the quicksand of the Colorado. The rear axle groaned and whined like a mortally wounded buffalo. The din was enough to rouse the sleepiest Mexican and by the time he reached the plaza a number of people had seen him pass, had cursed him in two languages, had shouted at him with a mixture of contempt and anger. He sat, straight as a lodge pole on the buck seat, unmindful of the taunts.

Not so Meredith Yancy, a sensitive youth with too much pride, who tried to appear small or disappear. The noise of the cantankerous axle boomed in his ears and he wanted to break up the wagon into firewood and send it up in smoke so he would never have to listen to its yammering din again.

The actual driver of the wagon, a man who worked for Mulejaw Wales, was asleep, or dead drunk, lying

49

atop the cartons of rifles. Hallman had not actually seen him drinking, but had observed that he was a peculiar man, erratic, toothless, and balding over most of his pate, with only slabs of gray hair above his jutting ears that he insisted was premature. He was a good driver and a good manager of the team of horses, for the most part, until every midafternoon when he began drinking suspiciously from a canteen and stuffing chunks of Climax tobacco into his toothless mouth and spitting gobs of juice all over the traces, the wagon, the seat, and himself. The driver's name was, he said, Charles Henry Chinaski, but everyone called him "Baldy."

Hallman had wanted to get his hands on the canteen and smell it, but Baldy slept with it tightly in his grip and it was always no more than a half-foot away from his hand ever since El Paso.

"Mr. Hallman," said Yancy, "I got a funny feeling."

"Yes, Yancy. Why is that?"

"These people here. Are they Indians?"

Hallman's nut brown eyes bulged in contemptuous indignation. He wanted to stop the cranky wagon, put on gloves, and beat the kid senseless. At least, smash some sense into his idiotic head. Meredith Yancy, to his way of thinking, was a raw spoiled brat who had inherited a ranch in Arizona and would probably squander its riches because he was, if not stupid, certainly ignorant of what it meant to be a man. The boy was not a man, and he was way beyond the age most boys became men. Twenty-five and thin as a rail, with that consumptive cough and bright glittery eyes blue as the pale shell of robin's eggs. Worse, he was an orphan: no daddy he could remember, no ma to give him any basic heritage to stand him in good stead.

Well, thought Hallman, the West would take the dandy out of him. Or kill him. That ranch in Arizona

Territory he'd inherited would make a man out of him or provide plenty of grave sites. The young man had money in his pocket, but it was money he had not earned. It was inherited money, which may have accounted for his condenscending attitude toward the others in the party. His parents had left him a tidy sum, but had wisley withheld the principal until he attained the age of twenty-five, perhaps suspecting that he might mature by that age. In this, they were wrong, but Hallman thought that the gift from Meredith Yancy's uncle might prove the better of the two inheritances. The ranch was not a trinket or a bauble, but a responsibility, something that despite its label was not a gift, but a treasure nonetheless—for the right person. The ranch would have to be worked, protected, nurtured, built up, defended.

Hallman smoothed his thatch of moustache and patted the pale duster that cloaked his Spartan frame. The duster looked rusty from the reddish powder blown onto its fabric, and the act was more a spit-and-polish habit than a practicality. The plaza loomed at the end of road and he saw the building Mulejaw had told him about, a tan adobe with a gate, bigger than the others nudged up next to it like clay bricks. His eyes narrowed above sharp high cheekbones, above the thin scar that creased the left one, a testament to a less-than-proficient skill at dueling when he was a callow youth much like young Yancy.

"That the place we're supposed to go?" said Meredith.

"You point like that all the time and women'll start to hang wash on your arm," said Hallman.

Meredith withdrew his arm violently as if burned.

"Colonel Hallman, you don't like me, do you?"

"I'm not a colonel anymore, Yancy, and I don't dislike you. I dislike your ways, your immaturity. A

51

man survives by observing, by using his brain. You know as much about our destination as I, yet you feel compelled to question your own judgment."

"I was just asking, Mr. Hallman."

"Don't pout, Yancy. You'll meet men in Arizona Territory who'll think you're a fop if you do that."

"Stop picking on me!"

"Ah, my young friend, a good point. No need to pick on you. You're doing well enough at that yourself."

Hallman wheeled the team up to the "livery" stable, the wagon protesting with metal shrieks that caused the horses to buck against their traces. He hauled in on the lines, stopping them from a sure bolt through the gate.

Yancy sulked until Hallman set the brake, wrapped the lines around the wooden handle, and stepped down.

Hallman walked to the gate and opened it. He peered into the dark interior of the makeshift barn. Scraping sounds grated on his ears. The sounds came from beyond the back doors. He opened the gate and walked inside. The smells of hay and grain mingled with the acrid aroma of urine, horses, and apples. The horses nickered and tossed their heads. He strode through, the smells strong in his nostrils. He opened the back door and heard it whine on its hinges. Light spilled into the adobe barn. A man looked up at him with pale gray eyes. The man had a knife in his hand and held a horse's hoof against his crooked knees.

Hallman drew up straight and stepped outside.

"I've brought a team in, and also a broken wagon," said Hallman. "Could use a hand when you get finished there. You're a blacksmith I see. Not a proper trimming knife, but you seem expert enough at it. Nice horse. Needs shoeing from the looks of his hooves. I didn't see a furnace inside." Hallman looked around. All he saw was a wide alley, and more small adobes cluttered beyond the empty space. "Someone let that horse go too long without being shod. I expected a Mexican in charge here, no offense. Heard there were white men in business here in Mesilla, though. You really ought to have those stables cleaned out, you know. Bad air. Bad for the horses."

Gunn looked at the man, sized him up. Military. Army, probably. Straight spine, square shoulders, trimmed brush under his lip. Not a prig, but not yet adjusted enough to civilian life to have dropped the authoritarian tinge to his voice. A major, perhaps a colonel. Trying hard to adjust to being out of uniform. He wore his pistol backwards, in a flapped holster. Cavalry. The man knew horses. Maybe he knew men, too. Certain types of men. Not this man.

"I heard you come up. Sounds as though your wagon needs more attention than your horses. You just make yourself to home," said Gunn politely. "I'm here same as yourself. Some Mexican kids'll be along shortly to help you with your team. I sent 'em up the *calle* to get some beans in their bellies. You'll have to haul your own water if your team is real thirsty."

"Sir, are you not the proprietor here?"

"No sir, I'm not. I'm just a traveler, like yourself."

"Do you know a man named Wales?"

Gunn dropped Esquire's foot and heard it thunk on the ground. He stood up straight.

"You must be Hallman."

"Yes, and who are you?"

"The name's Gunn."

"Gunn?"

"That's it."

Hallman's features tightened. His forehead wrinkled. Thick brows bushed over narrowed eyes as he looked Gunn up and down. Meredith Yancy came through the open door, a puzzled expression on his face.

"Mr. Hallman," said the young man, "what's the holdup? We going to unhitch those horses or what?"

"Meredith, a minute, please. I'm talking to this man."

"Oh, yeah. Hello, mister. Uh, sorry, colonel."

Gunn's lips bent on a wry smile. His eyes shimmered like a pair of dull silver coins.

"Gunn? Or is it Gunnison? Were you not a captain with the—?"

"Look, Hallman, the war's over. That one anyway. Mulejaw's at the hotel trying to get the ladies up. They've got *frijoles* and corn *tortillas* cooking at the cantina next door, enough black coffee to drown an army mule, and I'm trying to trim my horse's hooves until I can get him to a blacksmith. Nice meeting you and it looks like we'll be riding together for a spell in that old Concord."

It was a long speech for Gunn, but he wanted to keep Hallman at bay for a while. It was true that he had been a captain in the twenty-third Wisconsin and had fought at Missionary Ridge. People still talked about his charge and wanted to label him a hero, but he was a different man then, not only younger, but different in thought and bearing. A man did crazy things when he was pressed, when the stakes had a value that could only be measured by the situation. Looking back, he realized that he had been both foolish and lucky. He wanted no credit for killing good men who were also pressed, men who were also brave.

"I understand," said Hallman soberly. "I'll attend to my team, sir."

Hallman turned and started back inside the barn. Meredith Yancy stood there with his mouth open and Hallman had to stop, grab his sleeve, and yank the young man back to the task at hand. Yancy followed, reluctantly, turning to watch Gunn as he picked up his horse's leg and began cutting away the excess from the horny sheath of the hoof.

"Who was that man, Mr. Hallman?" asked Yancy, as they were unhitching the team. "He looked, well, different."

"Just a drifter, Yancy."

"Well he sure looks like he knows where he's drifting."

The ladies looked up as Gunn strode into the cantina.

Mulejaw Wales was just finishing up breakfast at another table, where he sat with two men, a Mexican and an American. He motioned for Gunn to join him. His bearded face wore a scowl.

"Ladies," said Gunn, doffing his hat.

"Good morning," they chorused. Hortense's eyes glittered. There were roses in her cheeks. They had finished breakfast and were lingering over coffee.

Gunn sat down at Mulejaw's table.

"Gunn," he said, "shake hands with Bert Munsey and Ignacio Delgado."

The introductions over, Gunn discovered the reason for Mulejaw's scowl. He spoke low, so that the women could not overhear.

"Bert runs the silver mine up at Stephenson's Peak. Ignacio's his overseer. Last night, they saw Jennings, Kelly, and the breed ride through. When they came back this morning, they had two dozen Apaches with them, painted for war."

"What do you make of it?"

"Ignacio here heard them talking. They were Sangre's band. He wasn't with them, but he's riding, stirring up the Apaches from here to the Gila."

"That is so," said Ignacio, a young man with a complexion the color of saddle leather. "They were talking about repeating rifles. Jennings, he say that they must wait until the right time."

"Which way did they ride?" asked Gunn.

"To Picacho, but one of the Apaches he say that Sangre is in Cooke's Spring."

Gunn's eyes narrowed. He looked at Wales.

"You know what that means?" asked Mulejaw.

"They won't hit you until you try and go through Apache Pass."

"Exactly," said Munsey. "You're crazy to ride into that. If I hadn't heard Jennings mention Mulejaw's name I wouldn't have known he was here. We had a double guard up all night. Damned Apaches were beating drums until dawn."

"They'll have some war party waiting for us, I figger," said Wales. "I been through that pass before when the Apaches were on the warpath. It warn't no pie social."

"I could send a man to El Paso, get on the telegraph," said Munsey. "Might be able to get some troops down here to escort you."

"Take too long," said Wales. "Hallman will want to go through. Besides, the army wants to sweep this way and clean out these Apaches with those Spencers. You couldn't get twenty troopers out of El Paso."

Gunn knew Wales was probably right. The army had abandoned most of its forts and were busy with Indians along the border. The Mexicans had put a bounty on Apache scalps, and the Apaches raided Mexico and holed up in the States. The Mexicans were hopping mad, but they had brought their troubles upon themselves. Still, the army was responding to political pressure to clean out the Apache renegades.

"Think we can get through?" asked Wales. "Have to

do it at night."

"I agree with Munsey," said Gunn. "Unless you have troops with you, it'll be rough, even at night. They can put Apaches all along that pass and it'd be like running a gauntlet."

"Here comes Hallman, we'll see what he says." Wales looked up. Yancy and Hallman came into the cantina. Yancy sat with the ladies who had been straining their ears to listen in on the conversation. Hallman sat down and shook hands with the men from the silver mine. Wales told him all he knew.

"It's a chance we'll have to take," said Hallman.

Gunn raked him with a searing glance.

"You've got women on that stage, Hallman," he said. "The Apaches won't show any mercy."

"I don't see that this is any of your business, Gunn. The ladies knew the risks when they bought their tickets. My job is to get those rifles through to Captain Rice."

"Jonathan Rice?" asked Munsey.

"The same. You know him?"

"He was at Fort Fillmore in '59. Good man."

"The best."

The *criada* served steaming plates of *tortillas,* beans, and steaks to Yancy and Hallman. Gunn took coffee. He had eaten before sunup.

"Can you give us any men?" Hallman asked Munsey.

"I'm sorry, no. They wouldn't go anyway."

"I would go," said Ignacio.

"Can't spare you. Besides, if Sangre gets his hands on those rifles, he'll hit every place along the road. He's let us know we're not welcome here more than once."

"He is a bastard," agreed Ignacio.

"Gentlemen," said Hallman, between generous bites of food, "we'll go through the pass at night. I've heard the Apache does not like to die at night."

"No, but he'll fight at night, just the same," said Gunn. "I should have killed Sangre when I had the chance."

"You saw Sangre?" asked Hallman.

"I didn't know who he was. He has a bad shoulder. At the time, I couldn't see shooting a man who couldn't defend himself."

"He would have shot you," said Munsey quietly.

Gunn said nothing. Hallman scrutinized him keenly, started to say something, and instead, wolfed down a chunk of steak, chewing it angrily.

"Well, that's that," said Wales. "Gunn, help me hitch up the team and we'll get started transferring those rifles to the stage. You come along when you're ready, Hallman."

An hour later, the stage was loaded. The springs sagged under the weight, but the old Concord was sturdy. It could carry nine passengers, a good amount of luggage, and two men on the driver's seat. Gunn hitched Esquire to the boot, threw his saddle and gear on the top, and lashed it down. The women had been given a choice of staying behind or going on. They had been told of the danger. Hortense talked to Janice and Amity, but they were too excited to stay behind and trust that Wales would come back for them.

"We'll go," she said.

"I'll teach you how to work the Spencer," said Hallman. "If you ladies don't mind shooting a savage."

"Big rifle for women," said Wales.

"We'd be delighted, Mr. Hallman," said Hortense proudly. She looked at Gunn, smiling. He was proud of her.

"Very well then," said Hallman. "Yancy, break open one of those cases and bring five rifles. Wales, throw me down a case of ammunition when you climb up."

58

"Aren't you going to ride in the coach with us?" asked Janice Longworth, dipping her eyelashes coyly. "We'd love to get to know you better."

Gunn's face flushed with color.

"I'd like nothing better, ma'am, but I'm riding up top."

"Girls, come along," said Hortense.

Gunn walked back to check Esquire one more time.

Hallman spoke to Wales privately.

"Wales," he said, "I think you're making a mistake bringing this Gunn along. Maybe he's in with Jennings and Sangre."

"No, I don't think so," said Wales. "What's bothering you?"

"I've seen him somewhere before. Or a picture of him. His name's Gunnison, I think."

Mulejaw cut himself a chunk of tobacco from a plug and tucked it into his cheek. He avoided Hallman's gaze and turned to climb up onto the seat. Yancy handed down brand-new rifles to Hallman, who put them inside the coach.

Gunn climbed up to sit beside Wales. He reached back, pulling his Winchester out of its scabbard.

"Gunn," said Wales, spurting a stream of tobacco juice out of the corner of his mouth, "you watch yourself. I think Hallman's done seen the same poster I seen back in El Paso."

"Not guilty," said Gunn softly.

"No, but they's a ree-ward offered by that Wyoming court."

"How much?"

"One thousand dollars."

"You interested in collecting it?"

"No sir, not me. I want to live to be a hunnert."

"Me, too," said Gunn.

The jehu kicked off the brake and snapped the traces. The team lurched against the straps and the stage rumbled away from the livery.

Beyond Picacho, they saw the first smoke of the day.

By now, every Apache along the old Butterfield stage route knew they were coming.

CHAPTER SIX

Mulejaw's old Concord averaged four and a half miles an hour over the rutted road. The blazing sun baked his and Gunn's backs until they were black with sweat. There were no smoke signals in the sky when they stopped to rest the horses a few miles out of Mesilla. The blue sky was cloudless; the land, red as a sunset, shimmered in watery dancing heat waves that blurred the horizon.

Wales watered the horses, Gunn helping him, while the passengers found places to relieve themselves out of sight.

"I could have shod your horse, Gunn," said Wales. "It would have set me back a half day."

"I know. I saw the shoes and blacksmith tools in the boot when I hitched up Esquire. But that's not the reason."

"No, I reckon not." Wales held a hide water bucket up to one of his horse's muzzles. "I seed the smoke yestiddy and knowed we was bound to have Apache trouble."

"Maybe your shoes wouldn't fit my horse. He's sixteen and a half hands high, has those Tennessee Walker hooves. The shoes you got back there look

61

more fitting for mules or these dray horses you set store by."

"Horses ought to be changed at Cooke's Spring, but that's fifty-one miles from here. A good twelve and a half, thirteen hours. Can't do 'er, so I carry my own tools, coal, bellows. Hell, I've carved shoes out of wood a time or two, hammered pasteboards two inches thick onto their hooves."

"And maybe used burlap soaked in potato paste once or twice."

Wales cackled. The water bag shook in his hands.

"Damn if'n you ain't been there."

"I was about ready to tack some of those hard *tortillas* onto Esquire's hooves, Mulejaw."

Again, Wales laughed. Then he turned serious.

"I knowed there was trouble when I seen that smoke. And Hallman's wagon goin' sour. My wagon. Now if Delgado says Jennings was travelin' with two dozen Apaches, I know he's maybe making it double or triple, but Jennings with any amount of renegade Injuns is medicine poor fer swallerin'. So, let's say Delgado saw a half-dozen Apaches with Jennings. That smoke says there's more. You're good with a pistol or long gun and you got good eyes to see Apaches what ain't there. Hallman, he's military. Dumb in his own way. The kid, he's wet behind the ears and too dandified to act quick. And, we got three ladies. So, I figgered my scalp might stay haired to my head a mite longer was you along. No hard feelings?"

"I was going your way," said Gunn.

He walked away from the coach, wiping his forehead with his bandana. He thought Wales would finish up his watering and call him back. Goatskins hung from the coach's side, bulging with cistern water, sweating like the inside of a cave. Enough, he thought, for animals and people, until they got to Cooke's Spring.

But Wales wasn't finished talking yet.

"Gunn?"

He turned around, saw Wales a dozen feet away.

"More?"

"Yeah. Hallman. He's a prodder. Won't give up on a thing."

"I figured so."

"He and Captain Rice are friends. Fact is, Rice married his daughter. She died and Rice volunteered for the worst the army had. Hallman likes the man and would go to hell for him. He could have had army people bring these blamed rifles, but it's a goldarned missionary thing with him."

"I savvy, Mulejaw."

"You be careful, hear?"

"Hallman's making money on this deal, too, isn't he?"

"Yeah," said Wales, walking away. "And he could use a thousand dollars."

Gunn did not have a chance to talk to Hortense. The young ladies, sweaty and discomfited by the heat, did not so much as glance at him when the stage was ready to pull out. Yancy, his face long and his temper short, stubbed his toe getting into the coach and glared at Wales with trembling lips.

"Just get inside, sonny," said Wales, "and be more careful next time."

"I want to talk to you at the next stop," said Hallman to Wales. "Private."

"Suit yourself, Mr. Hallman."

Gunn was glad he was riding atop the coach. The tension among the passengers was building to a critical point in the blistering heat.

"Haw!" yelled Wales, rippling the reins. The leather

cracked and the horses moved out, their hides sleek with sweat, the flies following them mercilessly, drawing blood despite the switching tails of the team.

"Here we go through the Pecatch!" hollered Wales above the thunder of hooves.

Picacho Pass was two miles of mountainous terrain. The hills made the going rough: they made the horses strain, made Wales curse, and made the coach groan like some dying beast when they reached the long stretch up to the summit. At the top, the broad and level plain stretched out below, empty, heartless, cruel, endless. It seemed, thought Gunn, that they would never get across it, and if they did, they would still be nowhere.

The Organ range dropped behind them as they descended onto the plain. Mesilla, ringed by the debris of the Rocky Mountains in a kind of lush amphitheater, was only a memory.

"That's Cooke's Peak you see," said Wales, pointing.

The peak rose from the plain in bold relief, jutting up above the surrounding hills. It danced in the waves of heat like a mountainous mirage, unattainable, worthless as the dirt between the pass and its foot.

The hours rolled by and the heat beat down on them until they were sodden rags swaying in the seat.

And, ahead, a smoke signal rose lazy in the sky like a small harmless cloud.

Wales picked an open spot, with shade, to rest the team, to let the passengers eat and stretch. Maria's lunch boxes were broken out—*tortilla* sandwiches with beef, sodden tomatoes, wrinkled potatoes, hard beans. It was food, but the young women complained that it tasted like pasteboard. The horses blew and swicked flies in the shade of a towering rock pile.

Gunn saw the coyotes before anyone else—gray shadows slinking through the brush.

"They smell the grub," he said.

"You got good eyes," commented Wales.

"Whatever do you see?" asked Miss Bangs.

"Coyotes," replied Mulejaw. "Be a good chance't for you to do some rifle practice Hallman. If'n the ladies are up to it."

"Anything would be better than sitting in this sweltering heat," said Janice. "And that coach is like an oven."

Hallman stood up, looking at Yancy.

"You could stand some practice too, Mr. Yancy."

Meredith's eyes brightened.

"Yes sir, want me to fetch the rifles?"

"One will do, and a box of cartridges."

Ned and Gunn cleared up the lunch debris as Hallman set up for target practice. He had explained the operation of the Spencer carbine to the women and to Yancy while in the coach. Now, he went over everything again, teaching them to load and aim.

Gunn got a rifle from the coach and held it to his shoulder. It was new, and like the others, had never been fired.

He worked the action.

"Ever use one?" asked Wales.

"We did," said Gunn. "This rifle probably helped us win the war. I was eighteen when I saw my first one, almost twenty before I got one for myself. But all through the war we kept hearing about the Henry. That's what everyone wanted when it was over, a Henry."

It was 1860 when the repeating rifle came into its own, especially the lever-action, tubular magazine version. Smith & Wesson took out its patent in April of that year on the rim-fire self-contained metallic cartridge. That was the signal for Spencer and Henry to take out separate patents on a mechanism to utilize the new cartridge.

Christopher M. Spencer was granted a patent for a cartridge breechloading repeating rifle that held the reservoir of bullets inside a tubular magazine inside the entire length of the buttstock. On the Spencer, the trigger guard served as a lever to advance the cartridges beyond the breechblock into the barrel chamber.

Benjamin Tyler Henry got his patent at about the same time. While his rifle utilized the same cartridge, and was a lever-action, tubular magazine-type weapon, he had designed his magazine so that it was located beneath the barrel, and the lever activated a carrier within the frame that lifted up the cartridges one at a time to align with the barrel chamber. A piston breechblock activated by the same lever extracted the empty shell and forced a new one into the chamber all in one cycle.

Spencer and Henry both had workable rifles, despite their minor flaws. Spencer was a better salesman, however. More aggressive, with better contacts in government. He petitioned Lincoln's administration to purchase a goodly number for the army. He demonstrated his rifle and the War Department, impressed, ordered a carbine version, eventually buying 100,000 units. Henry sat on the sidelines, but managed to get the War Department to buy a few of his carbines. He geared up for wartime production, certain that someone high up would see that he had the better rifle. Although only 1,730 Henrys were bought by the United States government, most of Henry's wartime stock was purchased by private parties, including soldiers in the field who had seen or heard of the Henry.

After the war, Spencer tried hard to grab a share of the civilian sporting-arms market with his carbine, but there were so many of his rifles on the surplus market he couldn't survive. He was competing with himself and with the Henry. In 1870, Spencer's company went under and was taken over by Winchester. The Henry Repeating Arms Co. thrived, however, and in 1866 became the Winchester Repeating Arms Co. of New Haven, Connecticut. When Henry and Winchester joined forces, they dominated the market. The Henry/Winchester's success prompted Colt, Whitney, and Marlin to bring out similar arms in the 1870s.

"Wonder why Hallman's bringing Spencers," mused Wales.

"These were probably made in '65 or '66," said Gunn, reading the barrel stampings. "Never used. He got 'em cheap."

"Wonder if Rice knows he's getting Spencers instead of Winchesters."

"I'm wondering if Rice is even in the United States Army."

Wales sniffled, tweaked his moustache, fluffed his beard.

"Now, Gunn, you got a point there. I wouldn't bring it up, was I you. My own recollection is that Rice and a couple of his men are regular cavalry, working with civilians who got tired of waiting for the army to do something about the Indians."

"Interesting," said Gunn, as the first shot from the Spencer boomed.

He and Wales walked over to watch the women shoot. Gunn tossed the Spencer in his hand to Yancy.

"Why, thank you, Mr. Gunn," said the youth.

"Try it out, if Hallman doesn't object."

"Load it up, Mr. Yancy," said Hallman, turning away from Hortense, who had fired the first shot. A white scrim of smoke hung in the dead air. She rubbed her shoulder.

"Did it hurt, Miss Bangs?" asked Amity.

"A—a little. Surprised me more than anything. It's sure loud, Mr. Hallman."

"Hold your mouth open when you shoot," he said, "and it'll be easier on your ears. One of you ladies want to try it?"

"I will," said Janice, stepping up.

"I see a coyote," said Yancy, when the Spencer magazine was full.

"Cock and aim, then," said Hallman.

The coyote was running through the brush seventy-five yards away.

"Lead him some," said Gunn.

Yancy swung the rifle and squeezed the trigger. A puff of dust kicked up a foot behind the animal. It stopped, started running the other way. Yancy levered another cartridge into the breech and fired again. The coyote, struck in the hip, twisted, yelping in pain.

"Better finish him off," said Gunn.

"Let Miss Longworth here try it," said Hallman. He helped adjust the stock to her shoulder after she cocked the rifle. "Just aim for the biggest part of the coyote."

Janice squeezed the trigger, and screamed.

"Ouch! That hurt."

"You have to hold the rifle snug," said Hallman, taking it from her hands. Her shot was high. The coyote twisted in circles, snapping at its hip. Hallman levered and fired quickly. The coyote's head jerked back. It crumpled and lay still.

"Good shot," said Yancy with admiration.

"Just try and think of that animal as an Apache," said Hallman.

A pair of coyotes, curious, padded toward the dead animal.

"Want a shot, Gunn?" asked Hallman, holding out the rifle.

"No. I see no purpose in shooting a coyote."

"What about an Apache? What about Sangre himself? Seems you winged him and then let him live."

"I did. He was out of commission."

"The only good Apache is a dead one," said Hallman, fixing Gunn with an accusing eye. "Isn't that what you figure, Gunn?"

"No. There are good Apaches and bad. This is their country. They've been hounded to death. Chased, run off, made to hide like hunted animals."

There was a long silence as everyone looked at Gunn, absorbing the heresy of his words.

"Why, Mr. Gunn," said Janice, attempting to dispel the tension, "don't tell me you like the savage Apache."

"I feel sorry for 'em," he said.

"Why, you scoundrel," said Hallman. "The Apache's a murdering, thieving, kill-happy cutthroat, impeding progress, holding back the settlement of the West. How can you justify letting them get away with murdering white people?"

"They were here first," said Gunn, walking away.

When he was out of earshot, Hallman turned to Wales.

"That's what I wanted to talk about, Wales," he said. "I don't trust Gunn. I think he's an Indian lover. Worse, he's a murderer."

The women gasped. Hortense's face drained of color as if slapped.

"I'd be mighty careful of accusing a man, was I you, Hallman."

Yancy stepped closer, curious. He looked off, saw Gunn walk to high ground.

"It came to me where I'd seen this Gunn before," said Hallman. "Not him exactly, but a picture of him. Back in El Paso. On a flyer in the United States Marshal's office. Gunn, alias William Gunnison, is wanted for murder in Cheyenne. He's been tried and convicted. He's a fugitive. The reward is one thousand dollars."

"Well, I'll be damned," said Yancy.

Amity tittered. Janice smiled. Hortense looked as if she was on the verge of fainting.

"I'd think twice before telling Gunn that to his face, Hallman," said Wales. "Could be that the man is innocent. Trial or no trial. Talk is that he was railroaded, took the blame for another man's crimes."

"I've heard that too, Wales. But I heard he worked for the Cattleman's Association up there and killed a lot of men in cold blood. For pay. That sounds to me like the man's a hired gunny. Right or wrong, he's a killer."

"What're you going to do, Mr. Hallman?" asked Yancy. "Need any help?"

Hallman glared at the youth.

"At the moment, nothing. I just think we'd all be well advised to keep our eyes on Gunn. He's dangerous. He may be in with a man named Jennings who's working with the Apaches. I don't trust the man."

"I trust him," said Wales. "That's why he's along. May come a time when you'll be glad he's with us."

"I doubt that, Wales," said Hallman, stalking away.

The old station at Cooke's Spring was abandoned, but there was a stone shelter and a big army tent set up. A man named Edgar Logan had a fire lit when the coach pulled into the clearing. He was a prospector who kept spare horses for Ned Wales. He brought a team down whenever the freight wagon was due. He greeted the arriving stage, limping out to stand with his back to the bonfire. He waved stubby arms, but hobbled out of the way after Mulejaw spotted him. Logan was a short, bandy-legged man with a clubfoot, his sagging belly partially covered by a long scraggly beard. He was curly headed and every hair was gray as sun-bleached bone.

"You're late, Mulejaw," rasped Logan. "'Spected you yestiddy."

"Late and eyes full of grit, but healthy as your old mule."

"Lickety-Split died last night."

"Died?"

"Died of a arrer."

"Damn you, Ed Logan, you're sure spare with the words. You sayin' an Injun shot an arrow into your mule?"

"Two."

"You have a fight here?"

"Not much a one. Lickety-Split got me out of it."

They switched teams while they pulled the story out of Logan through constant questioning. Eight Apaches had jumped him up on the rimrock while he was riding his mule back up to his camp after the horses. He had driven them off, but the mule had taken two arrows, and had to be shot finally.

"Any reason for them to jump you?" asked Gunn.

"They had paint smeared all over 'em."

"You see their smoke?"

"I read their smoke," said Logan. "Real plain."

"What do you make of it?"

"Sangre's gatherin' up all the Mescaleros and Mimbrenos for a big party over toward the Gila."

"Know where those Apache braves went?"

"I reckon Stein's Peak," said Logan. "Few hours ago, I seen more Apaches. Two white men with 'em."

"That'd be Jennings and Kelly," said Hallman.

"It war Jennings," agreed Logan.

71

Gunn looked at Wales in the firelight. The air was cool, fragrant with sage and scrub pines. It was a welcome relief after a day of sweat and dust and the hammering sun.

"Why Stein's Peak?" he asked Logan. "That's not much of a place for an ambush."

"No sir," said Logan. "It's jist a favorite camping ground for the Apaches."

"True," said Wales. "Chief Mangas used to go there. He always asked the station master there for corn and if he didn't get it, he would have taken scalps. Sangre's bunch'll think it's good medicine. There's a little hollow under the mountain where they'll have a party tonight less I miss my guess."

"I'm going back up in the mountains, Mulejaw," said Logan. "Soon as you pull out. Was I you, I'd go no further than right here. I set up the tent and you're welcome to it."

"We'll go on," said Hallman.

The ladies, sleepy, sat in the coach, listening to the talk. Hortense shivered in the chill and told the others to pay no attention.

"I'm sure Mr. Hallman knows what he's doing," she said.

"Well, if there's shooting," said Janice, "I want to be close to Mr. Gunn."

"But, you heard Mr. Hallman," said Amity. "He's a killer."

"Well, wouldn't you rather be with him than old blood-and-guts?"

"Hush up, girls," snapped Hortense. "Mr. Hallman might hear you."

"Well, I wish he'd ride up top and let Mr. Gunn keep us company," said Janice.

"Shameless," said Hortense.

"I wouldn't talk about being shameless if I were you,

Miss Bangs," pouted Janice. "Amity and I know you were in Gunn's room the other night. You didn't get back until dawn and—"

Hortense slapped Janice and then was immediately sorry. But now was not the time to explain. Besides, she didn't know how she could explain such a thing. All she knew was that whenever she thought of Gunn, she ached inside. Like Janice, she wished he was riding in the coach with them. She longed for him to touch her again, to hold her in his arms.

When the coach moved out, after midnight, she stayed awake a long time, her head resting against the corner, Amity sleeping with her head on her lap, Janice leaning her head on her shoulder. She finally fell asleep listening to Hallman and Yancy snoring on the opposite seat.

CHAPTER SEVEN

Mulejaw slept atop the coach while Gunn rolled the team toward the Mimbres River. There was not much water in it, but the horses drank in the dark. The canteens had been filled at Cooke's Spring and they wouldn't need water until tomorrow when they arrived at Soldier's Farewell. Seventeen miles west of the Mimbres, the stage passed through Cow Springs. It was deserted, and Gunn did not stop. They were in the center of the broad plain now and the air was warmer than it had been in the mountains.

The team ran well, making its four and a half miles an hour without strain. Gunn let them have their heads, and checked their direction by the stars. But the team knew the road and he had no trouble.

He knew they had been lucky so far. Had the Apaches not been superstitious, they might have taken the coach at any place along the road. But if they drew their medicine at Stein's Peak and had tasted victory previously at Apache Pass, that's where they would strike. He had no intention of letting Hallman push through there, day or night, with the women aboard, but he had kept his notions to himself. Ed would go along with him, he felt sure. Yancy had no mind of his own and would probably side with Hallman. As for the women, he couldn't allow them to have a choice. They did not know the danger. They did not know what the Apache would offer them if they were captured. They would be nothing more than slaves or concubines and lucky if not more was done to them than that. Likely, if Sangre won and carried out his plan, the white women would be used up and thrown away pretty fast.

Captain Rice evidently was a thorn in Sangre's side. If he read all the signals right, Gunn thought, Sangre would attack Rice's troops and then sweep back east to the Rio Grande, killing every white in his path. That would give him back much of his land. He would not be able to defend it, but he would sure as hell slow up settlement for a time. There would be a lot of blood spilled before it was over. Those damned Spencers. Worthless. The Winchester was a better rifle. Hallman was making money and people would die because of his greed.

If he had it figured right, Captain Rice was working outside the United States Army. Probably had taken a leave of absence and was charging the ranchers to lead them against the Apaches. So, he might prove to be another man of greed and poor judgment. If the army knew about him and what he was doing, that was one thing. But he doubted if they did. Something had sure as hell stirred up the Mescaleros and it was likely that Rice's bunch was responsible. The last thing this country needed was a band of white guerrillas operating in Apache country.

"Spell you, Gunn," said Wales, waking up shortly after dawn.

"All's quiet."

"That's what I don't like about it. We could run into Apaches at Stein's Peak, but I got a funny feelin' about Soldier's Farewell."

"How come?"

"That's the sweetest water on the plain."

Gunn slept soundly atop the coach, despite the bouncing. He pulled a tarp over his head to shut out the sun and lay his head on his saddle bags. He had slept in worse places.

The springs at Soldier's Farewell held a surprise no one expected.

Buzzards circled in a towering spiral over the site. Ned saw them well before the coach rumbled into the jumble of rocks that was the clearing where a tent had once stood. The ungainly birds flapped up in a dark cloud as he rolled the coach to a stop.

Gunn sat up, groggy with unfinished sleep.

"Somepin' bad," said Wales, holding his nose.

"Better tell the ladies to stay in the coach." Gunn scrambled off the top and swung down off the seat as Wales set the brake and wrapped the lines. Buzzards landed on the rocks, taking up positions, their silhouettes a grim reminder of their purpose. They ate only carrion. Dead flesh.

Gunn walked to the place where the buzzards had been feeding. His stomach churned when he saw the man staked out there. The eyes were gone. The eyes always went first. He was staked out, stark naked. The buzzards had already started to eviscerate him. Part of his liver lay over his crotch, buzzing with flies. Coils of slick shiny intestines lay like ropes over his abdomen. That was where the smell came from—not from decomposition. The man hadn't been dead that long.

He fought to keep down the bile that jetted up his throat. But he had to know. He knelt, touched one of the man's arms, and felt his neck. The flesh was soft. Rigor mortis was setting in, but the dead man was not yet stiff. They had made sure there was enough of him to recognize, the bastards.

Wales called over from the coach.

"What is it, Gunn?"

"Better come over here, Mulejaw. Bring Hallman with you."

Gunn stood up, and saw Yancy start over ahead of the other two.

"Better stay there, Yancy," said Gunn.

"I wanta see."

"Suit yourself."

Gunn looked at the dead man again. He recognized him.

It was the breed, Choya.

He had died hard, less than a half hour ago. He looked around and saw the coals from the fire. They were still smoldering. Half-burned faggots lay around the dead man. They had tortured him. Ugly burn marks scarred his body. His lips were scorched, blistered, running with blood and clear liquid.

That wasn't the worst part.

Choya's genitals had been burned and then hacked off, a piece at a time.

"Oh my God," exclaimed Meredith Yancy when he saw the dead man. He staggered away, retching.

Wales and Hallman came up and stood beside Gunn. They looked at the remains of the man Gunn knew only as Choya, the half-breed he had seen with Jennings and Kelly back in Mesilla.

"It's that damned breed," said Wales. "Now, why in hell would the Apaches do this to him?"

"Why would they do this to any man?" asked Hallman.

Yancy couldn't keep it down. He held onto a rock while he vomited. Wales looked at him in disgust.

"Look, son," he said, "do that somewheres else. We

got enough stink here."

Yancy, wild-eyed, tears streaming down his face, lurched away from the rocks. He wobbled toward the coach.

Hallman fought to keep from following Yancy.

"They wanted us to see Choya," said Gunn. "They wanted us to know they killed him. And before he died, they tortured him, not for pleasure, but because they wanted information. Look at his hands, his fingers. They started out on him slow. He must have held out a long time."

"Yeah," said Wales, sucking in air. "But why?"

Hallman looked up at the buzzards on the rocks. He unfastened the flap on his pistol, drew it, and cocked it. He fired at the buzzards in rapid succession, emptying the cylinder of the Remington .44. Explosions rocked the quiet. The acrid smell of black powder laced the air, covering up the stench of the dead man. Buzzards flapped away. One tumbled from its rocky perch and bounced down the face of a boulder. Its wings fluttered for a few moments as blood spurted from its headless neck.

"What'd you go and do that for?" asked Mulejaw. "They're just cleaning up a mess the Apaches left."

"You call this man 'Choya,'" said Hallman. "That was the name he used to gain the confidence of Jennings and Sangre. His real name was Eugenio Salazar. Sgt. Eugenio Salazar. He was one of Captain Rice's men."

Gunn's pale blue eyes turned slate.

"Are you saying Salazar was working for Rice?"

"Undercover. It took him a long time to get in with Jennings." Hallman kicked a dirt clod, then turned away from the spread-eagled dead man. "He provided Rice with valuable intelligence. We were able to know of Sangre's plans and his whereabouts. That's why Rice has been so successful in eluding capture."

Wales let out a long whistle.

Gunn tipped his hat back and scratched his head.

"So, they found out about Choya," he said. "How?"

"That's what I'd like to know," said Hallman.

Gunn wasn't finished with him.

"Hallman, you'd better let me know what we're in for with Captain Rice. Is he working for the army or on his own?"

"Gunn, you're way out of line. As a fugitive from justice, you're hardly in a position to demand anything of me."

"Maybe not, Hallman, but what Rice is doing, or trying to do, is wipe out a race of people. My own hunch is that the army doesn't know a damn thing about it. If they did, they'd reactivate Fort Fillmore and send out hunting parties in the heart of Mescalero territory. You're meeting him with these rifles in Pima country. The Pimas are blood enemies of the Apaches. You could have a full scale war on your hands if Rice gets the Pimas after Sangre, and a lot of innocent ranchers would pay the price."

"As I said, Gunn, this is none of your business."

"As of now, I'm making it my business. If Rice doesn't have the right answers, I'll take him down."

"That might be hard to do."

Gunn looked at him with nerveless eyes.

"I'll take you down as well," he said.

Hallman tensed. His pistol was empty, a useless chunk of metal in his hand.

"Better get on back to the coach, Mr. Hallman," said Wales. "Gunn and I will clean up this mess. You and Yancy can fill those canteens."

Hallman glowered, but said nothing. He turned on his heel and walked away.

"Thanks, Mulejaw," said Gunn. "I wondered, for a

minute, if he was going to start shoving bullets back into that pistol."

"He might at that. You got yourself an enemy, Gunn. Watch your backside."

They buried Choya, alias Eugenio Salazar, in a shallow grave some distance from the springs. The coyotes would get to him and then the buzzards would continue their interrupted meal. But what was left of the man was away from the water source.

"Dust to dust," said Gunn under his breath as he stacked the last rock over the grave. "And may God rest his soul."

"What was all the shooting about?" asked Hortense.

"Nothing," growled Hallman.

"Why did Mr. Wales take a shovel over there?"

"Look, Miss Bangs, you don't want to know. I've got to fill those bags, so when you finish, let me know."

The ladies were sponging off their faces with the cool water from the goatskins. Yancy sat in the shade of some rocks, pasty faced. Janice Longworth walked over to him.

"You look as though you've seen a ghost," she said.

"Next thing to it. A dead man."

Janice shrieked.

She came running back to Amity's side, and whispered in her ear.

"Is there a dead man over there?" asked Amity of Hallman.

"Yes, dammit. Yancy, you get over here, help me fill these water bags."

Wales had set out the folding canvas waterbags for the horses. They buried their muzzles in the water, blowing bubbles and sucking the liquid into their bellies. Esquire switched his tail, grinding his teeth as he tried to move the bit out of the way. The sound of the shovel could be heard beyond the pile of rocks.

Yancy rose from the rock and came over. He tried to stand up straight.

"I'd like to know what's going on here," persisted Hortense.

"I suggest you talk to Gunn. He'll be riding with you in the coach for a ways," said Hallman. "Yancy, are you well? I need some help."

"Who's going to drive the stage?" asked Yancy.

"I am and you're riding shotgun."

Yancy brightened. He did not look forward to the stuffy coach in his condition. His stomach was raw from the retching, his throat sore from the burning bile.

"I'd like that, Mr. Hallman."

"Come on, grab a water bag."

The women looked at each other after the two men left.

"We're going to have that old smelly Mr. Wales in the coach with us," said Amity.

"Well, I get to sit with Gunn," said Janice, her eyes flashing.

"Is that all you think about, Janice?"

"Not as much as you do, Amity."

"Girls, stop it. You'll behave like ladies. We'll sit in our regular seats and not bother the men."

"Speak for yourself, Miss Bangs," said Janice defiantly. "I'm just dying to learn all I can about Gunn. He's so handsome, so strong."

Amity's face darkened.

"Janice, you have no shame."

"Miss Bangs doesn't either. If she can do what she did I can certainly talk to the man."

It was Hortense's turn to get angry. She tried to control her temper, but grabbed Janice's arm and shook her. Janice shook off her grip and teetered off balance. Her shoulder struck the side of the coach.

"Ouch!" she exclaimed. "You hurt me!"

"I—I'm sorry," said Hortense. "It's just that you shouldn't talk that way. What I do is my doing and has nothing to do with the way you're supposed to behave. Besides, Gunn's too old for you, child."

Janice's blue eyes blazed. She shook her blond hair and took a stance, her feet wide, her hands on her hips.

"My mother told me something," she said. "'Better an old man's darlin', then a young man's slave.'"

Hortense lost all control.

She drew back her arm and flattened her palm. She swung. The flat of her hand struck Janice square on the cheek. Blood drained from the finger marks.

Amity rushed to her friend's aid, pushing Hortense aside.

"Don't hit her!" she screamed.

Hallman and Yancy looked over from the spring.

Janice backed away and started running.

"Janice! Come back!" Hortense started after her. Amity, fearing that Miss Bangs would harm her friend, lashed out, grabbing the woman by the dress. There was a ripping sound as the cloth tore.

Hortense stopped, looking at Amity in horror. Amity dropped the dress. It dragged in the dirt.

"You little hussy, get in the coach!" Hortense's face turned livid with rage. She picked up the torn end of the dress, and held it in her hand. She started to cry. Amity, chastened by what she had done, backed toward the coach.

Gunn and Wales came back at that moment. Hallman and Yancy shook their heads. They had seen the whole thing. Yancy had started to go over, but Hallman stopped him.

"Let them work it out," he said.

"That Miss Bangs is too bossy, if you ask me," said Yancy.

"Nobody asked you."

Amity opened the coach and went inside. She began crying too. Her sobs drowned out those of Hortense.

"What's the trouble?" asked Gunn innocently.

"Just look at my dress!" said Hortense. "Oh, I could choke Amity Heller."

"Where's Miss Longworth?"

Hortense looked around, a stunned expression on her face.

"Why—I don't know. She—she ran off."

"Better change your dress, Miss Bangs," said Wales. "We'll find the girl."

"It's not healthy to wander off around here," said Gunn. "Which way did she go?"

Hortense pointed. Gunn strode in the direction Janice had fled, shaking his head. Everyone's nerves were at the breaking point. Such things could be expected on a long hot trip, but this was no good. Jennings and the Apaches had left a warning. From here on, they could expect anything. Sangre might not be at Apache Pass. He could be anywhere. He could be watching them now.

Janice was still running when he caught up to her. She didn't look back and he saw that she was hysterical. He grabbed her arm, stopping her in her tracks. He spun her around. She looked up at him and swooned.

He caught her before she hit the ground, then held her in his arms as he crouched on bended knee.

"Miss Longworth," he said.

She moaned.

"Wake up, ma'am."

Eyelashes fluttered.

"Ma'am?"

He felt her trembling. Then, before he could respond, she rose up, throwing her arms around him. Her breasts mashed against his chest. She sought his mouth with hers, and planted a kiss on his lips. He struggled, but she kissed him even harder. He toppled over, the girl on top of him. She did not break the kiss.

Hortense Bangs found them like that.

"So, Gunn," she said, "you can't be trusted, can you?"

"Mummmpf," he said, trying to turn his head. He could feel Janice's loins on his, a damp heat soaking through him.

Hortense stalked up, grabbed Janice by her long tresses, and jerked her head back.

Gunn stared up at Hortense helplessly.

"I—I didn't—" he stammered.

"Shut up," she said. "I think you've done enough for one day. Janice, come on back to the coach and start acting like a lady."

Janice, subdued, shook her hair as Hortense released her. She looked back at Gunn longingly.

"'Bye," she said coyly. "I love kissing you."

Hortense gave her a shove.

Gunn got up and brushed himself off. He watched them walk away, then looked down for his hat.

He picked it up and crammed it on his head.

"Damn females," he said.

CHAPTER EIGHT

It was forty-two miles to Stein's Peak from Soldier's Farewell.

Gunn sat in the coach, drowsing, while Hallman drove the horses over the rough stretch. Mulejaw was asleep on the opposite side of the seat, his muffled snores barely audible above the rattle and rumble of the rocking coach.

Hortense had scarcely looked at him, and then only in a reproachful manner.

Gunn knew that no amount of explaining would make her understand that the Longworth woman had attacked him, not the other way around. In fact, if he did try to explain he would probably only make it worse.

Amity, not knowing what had happened, but knowing something had happened, had not taken sides. She and Janice had been whispering and giggling until Hortense had made them settle down. Now, both women looked at him with what he could only describe as bald-faced lust. He wanted to take Janice Long-worth by the short hairs and shake her until her teeth rattled, but that would likely be just what she wanted him to do.

He tried his best to ignore them, but Janice's bold looks, the way she wet her lips with her tongue, the way she jutted out her breasts, made her about as unnoticeable as a rattlesnake in a bedroll.

Amity, as if trying to outdo her friend, rolled her eyes at him whenever Miss Bangs wasn't looking and hiked her skirt up so that, as long as his eyes were opened, he was pretty well trapped. If he looked down, he saw Amity's comely ankles, and if he looked up he either saw Hortense glowering or one of the other of the two young ladies making eyes at him. The only other places to look were out the windows or at Mulejaw's bearded face in repose.

"Are you a killer, like Mr. Hallman says?" asked Amity.

"Hush, now," warned Hortense.

Gunn stared at Amity, wondering if Janice had put her up to that.

"Well? Are you?"

"Not in the way you mean," said Gunn.

"Mr. Hallman says you're a murderer."

"Please, Amity. Even if Mr. Gunn is not a gentleman as we thought, he has a right to his privacy."

Dust blew in through the open windows, but it was too hot to pull the shutters. Gunn was sorry now he had let Hallman take over the coach. But it wasn't his doing. Wales needed spelling. They had a long way to go before they came to the Gila.

He looked out the windows at the blue sky. The mare's tails were thicker now, and the dawn had been fire red. Unless he missed his guess, they'd be into weather before another day went by. The coach was rolling good, over the plain, and he figured they might get to Stein's Peak before nightfall, or shortly after. They had left Soldier's Farewell before noon or right at it, rolling out again after a hasty lunch two miles away

86

from the scene of Choya's murder.

"I don't believe Gunn would kill anybody who didn't try to kill him first," said Janice, rushing to Gunn's defense. "Would you, Gunn?"

"If I thought you ladies were serious," he said, "I might answer you."

"I'm serious," said Janice.

"So am I," echoed Amity.

Hortense snorted.

Gunn looked at both women. Gone was the look of frivolousness on their faces. They both seemed eager to hear what he had to say.

"I'm not a killer," he said softly. "Though some say I am. I have killed men when I thought I had good reason to use my gun. I don't hanker to take human life and if there was any other way out of it I'd never draw on a man."

"The taking of human life is never justified," said Hortense, forgetting her anger at Gunn.

"I won't argue that with you. I lost men in the war. Good friends. I killed men whose faces I never saw. I put away my weapons and took to ranching, tried to live close to the land, be a good neighbor. Some men in town got drunk, came out to my ranch and raped my wife. Beat her. Someone else shot her in the back. She died in my arms. There was no law there, other than what men thought they could get by with. It was Judge Colt and six jurymen."

"You took the law into your own hands, then?" accused Hortense. The girls stared at Gunn in rapt fascination.

"I hunted down the men who took my wife, who brutalized her. I gave them all a chance."

"Oh, my," exclaimed Amity, her eyelashes fluttering. "Did you kill them all?"

"No. I tried to bring them to legal justice. One man,

the leader, was tried and convicted. The others didn't hold with the law and tried to shoot me."

"But you've killed other men, haven't you? Besides those?" Hortense's voice was husky and her eyes glittered with a strange light.

"More than I'd like to say, ma'am, and now I'd like some of that privacy you mentioned."

He turned away to look out the window.

"Gunn," said Janice, her voice pitched low, "I think you're a good man. My father said that men were born killers and even good men had to fight the bad ones when the law was weak."

Gunn said nothing. If they did not know the West now, they never would. Their lives were in danger and if the Apaches attacked them, they, too, might have to kill.

It was after dark when Hallman eased the stage up close to the station at Stein's Peak. It was no longer used as a station, but it was still a wayfarer's stopover. Now, there were no signs of life. It was almost ten o'clock in the evening and the stars were hidden behind gathering clouds. There was a slow breeze that had cooled them down for the last dozen miles. The air was heavy with the promise of rain.

"Don't get down yet, Yancy," said Hallman. "We don't want to walk into anything we can't handle."

Yancy sat, the sweat on him cooling so that he began to shiver. He held the rifle in his hands, trying hard to peer into the darkness.

Gunn and Wales swung out of the coach. Both men carried rifles.

"I'll check it out," said Gunn. "Mulejaw, back me up."

"Step easy, Gunn. I'm right behind you."

The station was sheltered in a small hollow under the mountain. Gunn approached it, zigzagging slowly. He sniffed the air. No trace of wood smoke or Apache sweat. He walked a large semicircle and cut back across it to the stage, Wales about thirty paces behind him.

"Clean as a whistle," said Mulejaw. "Bring the coach on up to the corrals. We'll unhitch, and spend the night."

Hallman drove the team on into the hollow, and braked to a stop. He set the brake. Yancy and he swung down. Wales got a fire going some distance away from the corrals. It would give them light to see but not make targets of them.

Hallman didn't like any of it.

"I want to push on," he told Wales. "We're dropping too far behind schedule."

"Look, Mr. Hallman," said Mulejaw, "the horses need a rest. It's thirty-seven miles to Dragoon Springs. Ten of those miles are through Apache Pass."

A long silence.

The silence ate at them, like something hungry.

"I got things to do," said Wales, tired of shifting his weight from one foot to the other. "I need my wits and my wits is gone with worry and your pushing this team."

And Hallman let the silence stretch some more as if to wear the jehu down. Wales started to walk away.

"You rest some, Wales," said Hallman, "but this team had better be moving before dawn or I'll start cutting your fee."

"Don't threaten me, Hallman. I agreed to transport you to the Gile and no time gettin' there was mentioned."

"It's mentioned now."

*　　*　　*

"We'll have to stand watches," said Gunn, who had taken a torch and surveyed the ground around the station. "And sleep separate. The Apaches could come up on us in the dark. Make it harder for them if we're not all bunched up."

"Makes sense," said Wales.

"Who wants the first watch?" asked Gunn.

"I'll take it," said Yancy.

"Can you shoot? How are your nerves?"

"My nerves are just fine, Mr. Gunn. And I can shoot some."

"Well, just shoot up in the air. I don't want to die in my sleep from a stray bullet."

"Mr. Gunn, I don't mean to be disrespectful, but you act as if you're in charge here. I thought that Mr. Hallman was the boss here."

Gunn looked at the young man with renewed interest. Ned Wales sat on a rock, cleaning grime out from under his fingernails with the point of a Barlow knife. His head tilted and his eyebrows raised as he met Gunn's glance.

"Ned Wales is in charge," said Gunn. "We talked this over, since Hallman wanted to push on toward Apache Pass. We need our wits about us if we're going to make it through. And we need to make the coach safe as we can. You take the first watch, Mr. Yancy. Stay out of the firelight, keep low, and make no noise."

"I would think the high ground would be best."

"You'd be easy to spot."

"I don't know about making no noise. Seems to me we'd want them to know we're standing guard."

Gunn suppressed a smile.

"They know. You stay quiet and you'll hear them. If you don't hear them, you might get your throat cut."

Hortense gasped. She and the two young ladies huddled together next to a pile of boulders. Their faces flickered with firelight.

Hallman, who had been silent, standing off by himself, turned and faced Yancy.

"What Gunn says is sound," he said. "I'll take the second watch. I'll sleep over by the coach, Yancy. You wake me when you get tired—even if the two hours isn't up."

"Yes sir, I will."

"Do you intend for us to sleep separate?" asked Hortense. "I'm responsible for these young women."

Gunn turned to her, lurching away from the rock where he had been leaning.

"Suit yourself, ma'am," he said. "I'd stay under that overhang, which is probably the safest place. And I'd spread out so that it would make it harder for an Apache to see you."

Hortense blanched.

"I see. Amity? Janice?"

"I'm scared," said Amity.

"I think we ought to do what Gunn says," Janice sighed. "I don't want to be murdered in my sleep, either."

Distant thunder rumbled.

Yancy's pulse quickened. He looked around him, shivering in his thin coat. The fire quivered with wavering flames a hundred yards from his concealed position. He had a clear view of the camp. The coach was dimly outlined, the corral, the horses. He could not see the people sleeping, only shadows where he thought they might be. An hour had gone by and he tensed at every sound.

To the south he saw lightning lace dark clouds and moments later, the thunder reverberated.

He fought to keep his eyes open.

When he had volunteered to stand the first watch he had felt wide awake. Now, with everyone asleep, he turned resentful. His eyelids grew leaden and the firelight mesmerized him. He turned away from it and quickly looked over his shoulder.

He was certain he had heard something.

In the distance, a coyote yapped plaintively and he thought of death, shivering with the quiet, terrifying thought of dying young in such a lonesome place with no loved one to know where he was or where he would be buried.

Gunn drowsed in his bedroll, far from the others. His pistol nestled close at hand, a hard tool he hoped he wouldn't need this night. He heard the faint thunder and knew that they'd have rain before morning. It would slow them down, but it would also help them if it lasted long enough to see them through Apache Pass. Doubtful Pass they used to call it. Doubtful because when Mangas Coloradas, the Mimbreno Apache, rode, and the Butterfield stages were running, it was always doubtful if they could get through that narrow, ten mile stretch of hell. It would be no different tomorrow if Sangre had his braves hidden in the rocks and brush.

Sheet lightning illuminated the distant horizon. Seconds later, the angry rumble of thunder reverberated in the rock formations that bordered the station. Gunn opened his eyes for a moment, then started to close them. That's when he saw a silhouette of a figure coming toward him. The brief flash gave him only a scant glimpse of the dark shape. But it was moving and hunched over as if stalking him. His hand stretched out. His fingers closed around the butt of his Colt.

He drew the pistol and cocked the hammer back.

In the silence following the thunder, he heard the scrape of leather on sand.

This was no Apache coming for him.

A dark shape loomed over him.

"Hold it right there," said Gunn softly. "I've got a pistol leveled at your gut."

"D—don't shoot," said a quavering voice in a low whisper. "It's me."

The figure stopped. Gunn held the pistol steady. He did not recognize the voice.

"Who are you?"

The figure came closer.

"Amity."

Gunn hissed between clenched teeth.

"What the hell are you doing here?"

"Are you going to shoot me?"

"I ought to." He eased the hammer down and slipped the Colt back in its holster.

Amity dropped to her knees. Her hands sought his face. He tried to push them away. She crawled onto his bedroll and rubbed her feverish face against his.

"Woman, you're asking for trouble."

"Gunn, please, you don't understand. Someone— someone tried to crawl under my blankets. He—he tried to force himself on me."

He bolted upright. Amity clung to him. He reached out, touching her hands. They were trembling. Her breath was shallow, uneven. He sensed her fear, could almost hear her heart pounding. He grabbed her other hand, and squeezed them both.

"Suppose you tell me all about it," he said softly.

"I—I'm scared. I started to scream and he clamped his hand over my mouth. He—he forced me down. At first I thought it was you. He—he was strong. I—I could feel his—his thing. He had his fly open. It was

93

sticking out."

Gunn's thoughts raced.

Yancy was supposed to be on watch. Had he deserted his post? What about Wales? Could it have been him? Or Hallman? It didn't make sense. Anyone trying such a thing was sure to be found out.

"What happened then?" he asked.

"He—he told me to be quiet. He said he wouldn't hurt me. He put his hands on my breasts. He started to pull off my pantalets. I struck him. Then I rolled over and I kicked him. He rolled away and I ran. I couldn't scream. I knew it wasn't you, so I came over here."

"How did you know it wasn't me?"

"The lightning. When—when it flashed, I saw his face."

"And?"

"It was Mr. Hallman. He was the one."

"Jesus," said Gunn.

"I'm scared to go back there."

"I'll take you to where Miss Bangs is sleeping."

"No! I don't want her to know. I don't want anyone to know."

Gunn could understand that. She was ashamed. It was embarrassing. Hallman. He had misjudged the man. If Amity was telling the truth, that is. Well, a man could get ideas being out here like this. With three women in the party. Still, a man like Hallman, disciplined, should have more control over himself. He didn't like it. He didn't like it at all.

"You'll have to go back," said Gunn. "I'll speak to Hallman."

"No! Please!"

She threw her arms around his neck. Her breath blew hot on his cheek. He fell over backward as she pushed, as the full weight of her body struck his upper torso.

Amity began kissing him, peppering his face with her lips. Her kisses were like bee stings. Despite himself, he felt a stirring of desire.

Lightning flashed and he saw her as he pushed her away. Her bodice was low cut, her breasts riding up over the yoke. He saw her pantalets. The robe she wore was thrown open so that he saw her white undergarments lit for just a second.

"They'll skin us both alive, girl," he said. "Now get off me."

"I want you, Gunn. You did it to Miss Bangs and that's all that Janice talks about. She'd try it if she could, but I'm tired of hearing her talk about you."

"You're not in your right mind."

"Oh yes I am. That's all I've been able to think about. I'm just as much a woman as they are."

"Maybe, but you're not going to prove it to me."

"If you don't, I'll scream. I'll tell them you dragged me over here and forced yourself on me."

She dug her sharp fingernails into his shoulder. She straddled him, panting. He could feel her determination, sense the sweating desire that rippled through her loins. Her thighs quivered.

"Did you make that up about Hallman?"

She didn't answer.

"You did, didn't you?"

"I'm not going to go away. Not until you make love to me. I'm not kidding, Gunn. I'll scream and tear my bodice. I'll wake them all up and I'll go into a crying fit. Hallman will shoot you. Maybe Mr. Wales too."

She had a point.

Damn her.

"That's blackmail," he said.

"That's how much I want you," she husked.

She lay down on him, seeking his mouth with hers. He could knock her cold, drag her back to her bedroll. He could do a lot of things, but he'd spend half the night explaining. And, if Amity made good on her threat, Hallman just might shoot him. Yet he didn't like the idea of a young snippet like Amity forcing him to act on her wishes.

"Will you go back if I do this thing?" he asked.

"Yes. And I'll never breathe a word to anyone."

"You're a bitch," he growled.

"I know," she breathed.

CHAPTER NINE

Amity snuggled against Gunn, her eager body pressing against his.

Her smothering scent clogged his nostrils, stirring his senses. Her mouth smeared a trace of dampness across his lips, and mashed against them with a sensuous quivering pressure.

"Ummm," she moaned. Her hips and thighs ground against his. He felt her heat through the cloth of their garments.

His manhood hardened, bulging against the crotch of his trousers. He felt her breasts flatten against his chest. He shot his tongue into her mouth, and probed the steam-hot dankness. Her tongue rose up to meet his, tangling with it savagely. A stab of desire tugged at his loins.

He broke the kiss and rolled over, bringing her next to his side. She gasped, squirming as he gazed down at her in the dark, his hands gripping her sides firmly.

"Amity," he said, "you sound bold, but are you sure you know what you're doing?"

"Yes, yes. Oh, Gunn, I'm so excited. I'm thrilled to be with a man like you."

Light washed over her face as jags of electricity laced

the dark clouds in the distance. He looked into her glittering eyes and saw the woman behind them. He saw the smoldering desire deep in her pupils, the raw lust frozen and magnified on her face for that split second when lightning brought her features into sharp relief.

He stripped her out of her low-cut camisole and tucked it under her head for a pillow. Then he slid off her pantalets, easing them down her legs. Those, too, he wadded up and stuffed under her head. He sat up, peeling off his shirt, wriggling out of his trousers. She sat up and took off her loosely laced high-top boots with trembling fingers.

Naked, they embraced each other, flesh melding into flesh. Their mouths joined and his hand kneaded one of her firm young breasts, his fingers teasing a nipple. The nipple hardened to a rubbery elasticity. She writhed against him and moaned.

"I have no experience," she confessed.

"That'll come soon enough. Do what you feel like."

"I don't even know what to do first."

"Just follow me, then."

He kissed her, touched her breasts, caressed her tummy. His hand nestled between her legs, and he stroked the fine hairs that grew thickly over her sex. His finger plied the labials and poked into the oil-slick portal. She jumped as he touched a tender muscle, then embraced him as a shudder passed through her.

Her hands flew over his body like errant birds, squeezing and stroking the hard cords of his muscles. Her back arched as she pulled herself up to him, ringing his neck with her arms. Her mouth was wet and open. He tasted her, tasted crushed mint.

"Ah," she sighed, sinking away from him. "I'm burning up."

"That's part of it."

"Gunn, do you like me?"

He almost laughed. She was serious. He did not laugh.

"I like you."

"You're not mad?"

"I ought to be."

"But you're not."

"Lord, woman, I'm too far gone for that. I'm burning up too."

She laughed nervously and he smiled in the dark, a dark flickering with lightning flashes every few seconds.

He bent to her, kissed her hard, pressing his loins against hers. His rock-hard cock burrowed between her legs, pushed against the lips of her sex, and slid up to the bony mound above the damp, yielding crease. Hot fluids seeping from the eyelet of his penis soaked into her skin. She winced with pleasure, and coiled a leg over his hip.

"Yes," he said into her mouth, "like that. You can do anything you want, Amity. Anything you feel like doing."

"You don't know what you're doing to me."

"No."

"It's good. I feel all warm inside. Happy. Like I'm melting. Like there's a fire deep inside me."

"It's the same for me, Amity."

"It is?"

"Yes. The same."

He showed her that it was. Hungrily, he began to roam her face and neck with his mouth. He flicked his tongue inside her ears, sending shivers through her body. He kissed her breasts, laving the hard nubbins of her nipples with his tongue tip. She turned into a writhing, sinuous animal squirming beneath him. Again, his hand dove between her legs and fondled the

99

furry nest of her sex. He probed the swollen lips of her pussy; his finger penetrated to the little nub-trigger of her desire. She jerked, and gasped. Her body undulated with a quick shuddering tremor. She bit into his shoulder. He tickled the tiny trigger inside her again and she flooded his finger with a gushing freshet of hot oil.

"Yes, oh yes," she whispered, her voice husky, rasping. "Now I know, Gunn. I truly know."

But he knew that she did not know. Not yet. She would, though, once the woman in her had been tapped, released. It was there, the womanness of her, untested, dormant. Waiting to emerge, full-blown. Her body was lean and lithe, her belly taut, slightly mounded. Memories of his dead wife, Laurie, came back to him—the first time they lay together as man and wife. Sweet, poignant memories of a young girl transforming into a woman: eager, inexperienced, loving. He wished that Amity had found her own man, her own young love, but he knew that love between a man and a woman found its own way, in its own time. Desire did not know of age or experience. It happened without plan or pretext, mostly. It happened anywhere, at any time. It could happen during a war, on the battlefield, in the middle of a lonesome prairie, or during a time of grieving.

It was happening now, during a time of danger, under the threat of a storm, in a camp full of strangers.

As he grappled with her, he wished he could see her face, see the wonder in her eyes. Suddenly he felt very tender toward this wayward lass, this hungry child-becoming-woman. She had come to him and he'd tried his best to turn her away even though most men would have jumped at the opportunity, if the consequences were not too severe.

Gunn was well aware of the customs and moral

standards of his day, the rigid Victorian morality that had shaped a girl like Amity. Shaped her, but not imprisoned her, evidently. He had once been bound by similar restrictions. Society's restrictions. The trouble was, he had learned, society was a shapeless, adaptive abstraction out West, on the frontier. Men had left the safety and comfort of New York or Boston or Philadelphia and passed through bewildering frontiers where the country and the times and the people all behaved according to new codes, new morals.

He had seen women widowed, by Indians or other white men, who suddenly wanted to make love even before their husbands were cold in the ground. He had seen good men come in out of the wilderness and stand in line to lie with the only whore in a settlement. He had seen men fight to the death over a fat, homely squaw, whose hair was infested with lice and whose skin was oily with the sweat of those who had lain with her before, whose loins carried dripping disease and worse. And he had seen refined, cultured women from the East turn wanton and savage once they had thrown off the shackles of civilization and tasted the heady air of freedom out West.

Customs and morals offered protection in a close-knit, self-regulated society. But they were of little use in a land where a man might not see his nearest neighbors for a year, where vast lonely stretches of desolate country stripped off civilization's veneer in a single season.

Amity, he knew, was not a bad girl. In another place, she might be branded immoral, loose, meretricious. Yet here, now, she was merely responding to a common human hunger, a hunger such as happened during times of danger, or stress, or isolation. Tomorrow, Amity might be dead. He, too, might die from an Apache bullet or a war club. Society had no power here. Civilization had no influence on a warrior's arrow or a rifle's bullet. Civilization was back in El Paso, or ahead in Los Angeles or San Francisco. It was not here on this lonesome peak in the middle of nowhere. Here, in the Chihuahuan desert, the human heart beat savagely. Here, the blood pulsed to a different, more primitive, rhythm. Here, there was only lawlessness and peril. Here, too, was raw lust and a boundless human spirit that throbbed with a single driving force: survival.

Gunn caressed Amity tenderly, lovingly, smothering her in his strong arms. He kissed her face, lingered on her lips as his loins locked on hers. He rose above her, and slid past the swollen labials into the spongy heat. She shuddered as he sank his shaft, plumbing her virginal depths. She stifled a cry and raked his back with desperate hands. Lightning flashed and bathed them in an eerie light. He stroked her, battering her maidenhead with soft rams that weakened the membrane.

"Don't scream," he whispered.

"No—no, I won't."

Her body bucked with a sudden ripping spasm. She bit her lip to keep from crying out.

A roll of thunder drowned out their thrashings as Amity quickened, her orgasm coming with an involuntary shudder. She mewed his name over and over as she climaxed again and again.

Her pussy was tight around his swollen cock, clasping it, squeezing it like a palsied hand.

He held back, slowed to keep from exploding his seed inside her. Still she quivered and shook. Her moans drifted from her slack mouth. Her loins smacked into his as she pushed upward, legs spread, feet flat. The blankets slid from Gunn's back and he felt cool air on his sweat.

"Deeper," she pleaded.

"Soon, Amity."

"I want it all, all of it."

He hammered the tough membrane of her hymen. He felt it stretch and loosen, but it held fast.

"More, more," she begged.

Her hands rubbed up and down his sweat-sleek arms. Their loins smacked together noisily, sounding like the clack of wooden sticks. The thunderclaps sounded closer and jagged streaks of lightning scarred the dark clouds only a few miles away.

He burrowed deep in a plunging dive just as Amity thrust upward with her hips.

She gave a sharp cry as her maidenhead sundered.

Her fingers raked his sides. He plunged past the torn shreds of her virginity clear to the mouth of her womb. He sank into hot seas and felt the lava rush of warmth flood his shaft. Amity thrashed with a series of climaxes. Her legs quivered. Her loins undulated, out of control.

"Oh, Gunn," she whispered. "I never knew it would be like this—so beautiful."

She bucked again and again, urging him with her body to keep plumbing her depths. He stroked her faster and faster until his juices boiled, bursting free of his sac. He squeezed her hard as his ejaculate squirted, as his manhood died the little death.

Thunder boomed and lightning lanced a high rock, striking sparks.

The rains danced across the land, reaching them with a silver curtain of needles.

He clasped her to him as he rolled off her body. She pulled up the blankets and clung to his warm flesh, shivering, not from cold, but from the aftershocks of pleasure.

Sometime later, Gunn dug out his slicker and gave it

to Amity. She put on her pantalets, camisole, and boots, and stole back to her bedroll. He watched her leave with sadness. He slept fitfully, waking reluctantly when Ned Wales shook him.

"Time to go," said Mulejaw. "It'll be slow in the mud."

Gunn sat up. He was soaked. He blinked, saw the fire blazing.

"I allowed time to dry out," said Wales.

"Coffee on?"

"The coffee's boiling and everybody's asking how Amity come by that slicker she's wearing."

"Shut up, Mulejaw."

Mulejaw grinned as he hobbled away toward the fire.

Gunn gave Amity credit. She didn't come right out and say she'd been in his bedroll. But her cheeks glowed and her eyes glittered. Hortense knew. So did Janice. Yancy shivered by the fire, soaked to the skin. Hallman stood watch in his slicker.

"Time to load up and move," said Wales, pouring the last of the coffee on the fire. He shoveled dirt over it. The women watched it sputter. A faint line of light appeared on the eastern horizon as Gunn and Wales finished hitching up the team. Hallman walked in from his post, rifle crooked in his arm.

"Quiet," he said.

"And wet," said Wales.

"Save me any coffee?"

"There's a cup on that rock over there," replied Mulejaw. "Bring it with you. Gunn and I'll haul us to Dragoon Springs."

Hallman headed toward the rock where the tin coffee cup steamed.

"Talk to you a moment, Gunn," he said. "Private."

Gunn looked at Mulejaw. The jehu shrugged. Gunn

walked away from the coach a few paces behind Hallman.

Hallman picked up the cup of coffee and blew on it before drinking.

"What's on your mind, Hallman?" Gunn watched the man carefully. The ex-army man held the Spencer loosely in one hand, drinking with the other.

"I'm going to make you an offer, Gunn. My advice is to take it."

"That's pretty good. Advice and an offer, all in one shot."

"I'm serious."

"I've had offers before. And I get free advice all the time."

Hallman frowned. So far, it was not going his way.

"I'd like you to go your own way. I'll pay you two hundred dollars if you'll stay at Stein's Peak and let us go on without you."

"Any particular reason?"

"I don't like you, Gunn. I don't trust you."

"The feeling's mutual, I reckon."

"I'm making you a reasonable offer. I don't want to go through that pass and have to watch my back."

Gunn didn't buy it. His pale blue eyes were gray smoke as the eastern horizon continued to pale. The sky was still overcast, the clouds low, threatening. The air had a fresh smell to it, like laundry on a line. It was cool.

"I have no reason to kill you, Hallman. Not yet."

"You've killed before. You're a wanted man. There's a reward on your head."

"So you think I might kill you because of that?"

"The thought crossed my mind," said Hallman.

"I've paid my fare. I'll go on to the Gila."

Gunn started to leave. Hallman stepped in his path.

"I'll buy your horse, give you one of the team. Three

105

hundred dollars."

Gunn sucked in a breath. He looked over at the coach. Ned was sitting atop it, looking his way. The horses were stamping their hooves, impatient. Esquire shook his head, fluttering his mane.

"You must want me out of the way pretty bad."

"I just don't want more trouble than I've already got."

"You won't get any trouble from me, as long as your brand is legal and your tally's right."

"Meaning?"

"You figure it out, Hallman."

Gunn walked away, listening. If Hallman so much as started to cock that Spencer, Gunn intended to kill him in his tracks. He had gone several paces when Hallman fired his last salvo.

"I saw who shared your bedroll last night, Gunn."

Gunn turned. His eyes were cold, dull as old nickels.

"You say one more word, Hallman and I'll put a lead ball where your mouth is."

Hallman's face drained of color. He drank his coffee, peering at Gunn over the rim of the cup. Gunn waited, then turned on his heel. He swung up to sit beside Wales.

"What was that all about, Gunn?"

"I think Hallman's made a deal he doesn't want me to know about."

"The rifles?"

"Maybe. I don't think he ever intends for Rice to get his hands on those Spencers."

Wales worried his chaw from one side of his jaw to the other. Hallman walked to the coach and opened the door. He climbed in and slammed the door.

"I don't get your drift, Gunn," whispered Wales.

"Could be that Hallman knows Jennings better'n we thought."

"You ain't sayin' he's selling these rifles to the Apaches?"

"I hope he's not. For some reason he wants me out of the way, and he picked this time to make it known."

"Right before we got through Apache Pass."

"Get the team up and the coach rolling, Mulejaw. I can hardly wait to see what's up ahead."

"Jesus the Christ, Gunn. I think you've gone plumb loco."

Wales took off the brake and riffled the reins. Gunn turned around to inspect the crates of rifles. The team took up the slack in the traces and began moving onto the trail. It was all downhill, but a few miles ahead, Apache Pass waited.

The rifles seemed to be all there in the crates.

Maybe he was wrong, Gunn thought. Maybe Hallman just didn't like him, as he said.

Still, he couldn't help wondering why Rice would want Spencers when he could have Oliver Winchester's 1873 lever-action. Every time he added it up, the answer came out wrong.

CHAPTER TEN

Apache Pass was narrow, bordered by perpendicular rocks that looked as if they were about to fall should anyone pass. The rocks offered concealment. The old stage station lay just beyond the ten-mile stretch.

Wales pulled up and looked at Gunn just before they entered the narrow defile.

"What do you think?" he asked.

"Mighty quiet."

"I don't like quiet like that."

The sun was hidden behind clouds. There was no glare. Gunn scanned the rocks, looking for anything that moved. Nothing moved.

"They might let us get well inside, then hit us."

"I've run it before."

"Well, run it now. Don't stop. I'll tell everyone to get ready."

Gunn swung down and opened the side door of the coach.

"We're going through the pass. Hallman, you ready?"

"Ready. Yancy and Miss Bangs will fire out the left windows. The young ladies and I will take this side."

"We're going hell-for-leather," said Gunn. "Stay low and look high."

He slammed the door shut, trying to blot out the faces of the women. They were scared. Their faces looked as if they had been dusted with flour. Yancy looked peaked, too. Only Hallman seemed calm, prepared.

Gunn climbed up, checking his Winchester. He dug out a box of shells and put them on top of the coach between two suitcases. He opened the box, rattling the bullets.

"Ready, Mulejaw."

"Hoo Haw!" yelled the jehu, cracking the whip. The coach slithered through slick mud, gained momentum, and straightened out. The horses strained at their harness and started through the pass.

Gunn's eyes roamed the high rocks on both sides of the pass. Suddenly, he tapped Wales on the arm.

"Pull 'em up!" he shouted.

"Whoa! Whoa there!"

The coach slowed. Mulejaw looked at Gunn for an explanation.

Gunn pointed behind them. A puffball of smoke rose in the sky.

"Save the horses," he told Wales. "That's what they wanted us to do—hit the pass running and the team'd be tuckered out by the time we reached the end of the pass."

"By Gawd, I think you're right."

More smoke rose into the sky.

"No sun, so they couldn't use mirrors," said Gunn. The team slowed to a walk. Hallman stuck his head out the window and shouted up at Gunn.

"How come we slowed?"

"Just take it easy, Hallman."

"What's that smoke I see?"

"Don't worry about it. You just stay ready down there."

Hallman started to say something, but thought better of it. He pulled his head back inside the coach. The murmur of voices drifted up to Wales and Gunn. The women were excited; Yancy, too, from the pitch of his voice.

There was no answering smoke at the other end, but Gunn knew they were there.

"We'll be up to our asses in Apaches," said Wales.

Gunn nodded. He levered a shell into the chamber of the Winchester .44. He eased the hammer down to half cock. There was no way of telling when the attack would come, but his guess was that they could expect to be fired at anytime past eight or nine miles into the pass. He and Wales were likely targets for the first bullet.

His stomach knotted and fluttered.

The coach seemed to be crawling along the road. The horses were nervous, itchy to move out. They didn't like the rocks and Ned had his hands full keeping them in check. The lead horses wanted to spook, despite their blinders. The talk from the coach died down. A silence rose up, punctuated only by the clop-clop of the horses' hooves and the snap of traces. Mulejaw leaned forward in the seat, working the tobacco in his mouth.

The minutes flowed by. Four miles and no sign of an Apache.

"I'm gettin' a mite nervous," said Wales.

"Stay that way. I tell you to move out, you hunker as low as you can and whip hell out of the team."

"Just say the word."

Another mile. Five miles into the pass.

Gunn ticked off the miles, judging the feet in quarter-mile segments. By the time they were eight miles into the pass, they still had not seen any sign of Indians. Wales grew more nervous. He looked at Gunn, his eyebrows arching. Gunn shook his head. He marked another half mile.

"Now!" said Gunn.

Wales cracked the whip over the team. The coach jerked as the horses hit the traces. The stage rumbled over the muddy trail.

A small puff of smoke appeared next to a column of rocks. A second later, they heard the crack of a Henry. A bullet sizzled overhead.

Gunn dropped to one knee and fired at the place where he had seen the rifle smoke. Wales hunkered low, yelling at the team. He snapped the reins, whipping the backs of the horses. Their manes and tails flew in the wind as the coach roared down the grade at full tilt.

Rifle snouts appeared from behind rocks. Rifles boomed. Bullets whistled, then thunked into the stage. Gunn saw an Apache stand up to take aim. He tracked the figure and squeezed the trigger of his Winchester. The Apache dropped like a stone, his rifle clattering on the rocks.

The people in the coach started firing. There were Apaches on both sides of the pass. Gunn counted a half dozen, saw a half dozen more bunched up in the rocks ahead. He fired and reloaded.

An Apache fell in front of the coach. The horses shied, veering off of the narrow trail. Ned Wales fought to keep them in line. A rifle cracked close by and Gunn heard the sound of a bullet thunking into flesh. He turned, and saw Ned sway sickeningly in his seat.

"Caught one," muttered Wales.

"Hang on, Mulejaw."

Gunn looked up, and saw a shadow. He tried to swing his rifle. More shadows jumped from the rocks, landing atop the stage. An Apache swung a war club, striking Gunn in the shoulder. Another fired into Ned's back at point-blank range.

Apache war cries filled the air.

Painted warriors clambered onto the stage. Gunn dropped his rifle, turned, and grappled with a painted brave. While he struggled, two braves began cutting the ropes that held the luggage atop the coach. Another leaped past Gunn and grabbed the reins. Ned Wales fell sideways in a slump, blood oozing from a hole in his back. Gunn's shoulder throbbed with pain. The Apache was strong, and had the advantage of being above Gunn. His hot breath blew against the gray-eyed man's face. He felt his left shoulder drop, weakened from the blow by the war club.

The team slowed as the warrior hauled in on the reins. Two other warriors who had jumped atop the coach began breaking open the rifle cases. Shouted Apache words brought braves riding fast on ponies. Gunn saw them out of the corner of his eye. The coach came to a full halt. The firing from inside the coach died down. Apaches grabbed rifles and ammunition as they rode past.

The Apache forced Gunn back. He pushed, then released. The Apache fell toward him, off balance. Gunn swatted him with his forearm, sweeping him off the seat. He reached for the Winchester, but the brave holding the reins turned and drove a fist into Gunn's belly. The wind flew out of his chest. Pain ranged from his solar plexus to his spine. The Indian swam before him.

"Es todo!" yelled an Apache atop the coach.

"Saca los cartuchos!" said another, both speaking in Spanish.

"Cuidado con el gringo adentro."

"Aquel Hallman. *No le molesta."*

Gunn warded off blows from two Apaches. He heard

a woman sobbing and a moment later a man's groans from inside the coach. The Apaches leaped onto ponies brought up expertly by their companions. He heard the click of rifles being loaded. The last Apache kicked him in the groin and leaped over his back onto a pony.

Gunn doubled up in pain.

Shots came from inside the coach. An Apache, turning, fired at him, but the bullet thunked into the footrest, splintering the wood. Through pain-smeared eyes, he brought up the Winchester, and sent a shot sizzling after the last brave.

The hoofbeats faded away.

A heavy silence settled over the pass.

Gunn slid the rifle down his leg and leaned it against the seat. He grabbed Ned by the shoulder and pulled him up from his slump. Even as he did so, he knew he was pulling dead weight. He turned the teamster over, and looked into glassy eyes that would never see again. Blood had stopped pumping through the holes in Ned's chest, one an entrance, the other an exit wound.

A coach door opened with a loud creak.

Meredith Yancy walked to the front of the coach, looking up.

Gunn looked down at him.

Yancy's face was dotted with powder burns. A trace of blood marked a crease on his forehead.

"Is he—?"

"Dead," said Gunn. "How about—"

"God, they killed Miss Bangs. And Hallman's got a bullet in his shoulder."

"The misses?"

"All right, I think."

Gunn laid Ned out on the seat. He jerked a tarp off the top of the coach and spread it over the dead man.

"I'm going to hand you some tack, Yancy. Stack it alongside."

"Yes, sir."

Gunn threw his saddle and gear down, then found bridles. Someone would have to ride bareback. The coach was jammed into a pile of rocks, the left wheel broken. Three spokes had cracked, and the rim was bent. They would have to ride out on horseback and leave most everything behind.

"Help us," came a cry from the coach.

Gunn swung down, wincing as pain flooded through the muscles of his shoulder. He had been lucky. That blow might have taken his head off. The pain in his scrotum was diminishing, but he walked gingerly to the coach. He looked through the open door.

Yancy stepped up behind him.

Janice held Hortense Bangs in her arms. There was a red stain over the dead woman's heart.

"Did she suffer?" asked Gunn.

Janice looked at him with tear-filled eyes, and shook her head.

"You and Amity step out. I'll take care of her."

Gunn's eyes shifted to Hallman. Hallman stared at him with eyes dulled with pain. He held a hand to his shoulder, covering a wound. His hand was bloody. His face was chalk white.

"You hurt bad?" asked Gunn.

"I'll live. Medicine kit topside."

"I'll fetch it," said Yancy.

Gunn helped the young ladies from the coach. Amity was dumb with the presence of death, trembling. Janice seemed more composed, but her face was drained of color. Their hands were begrimed from handling the Spencers and the ammunition. Their dresses were rumpled, their hair askew. They looked, he thought, like moppets, orphans.

"What will happen to us?" asked Janice.

"We'll get out of here, go to Tucson," said Gunn. "First, there are things to be done."

"What about Miss Bangs?" asked Amity.

Gunn looked at her, saw her eyes misting.

"I'll see to it she's laid out. Have to send a wagon back to pick up her and Wales."

"He's dead, isn't he," said Janice. It was a statement.

"Yes."

Gunn stepped into the coach. Yancy appeared a few seconds later with a medicine kit.

"Let's take a look at that wound," said Gunn. He drew Hallman's hand away. The bullet had torn through the flesh, but had missed the bone. There was a lot of blood. He took off Hallman's coat and ripped his shirt away from the wound.

The medical kit was in a leather bag. Gunn found alcohol, swabs, various ointments, bandages, surgical instruments. The satchel was the kind carried by army surgeons in the field. He laid out the things he needed, and began to dress Hallman's wound. He poured alcohol into the chewed flesh. Hallman, seized with pain, closed his eyes, wincing. Gunn ran a swab through the wound after dipping it in antisepsis lotion. Hallman lost consciousness.

Swiftly, Gunn packed the wound with a medicated salve and bandaged it. Hallman did not come to.

"I'll cut him a sling," said Gunn to Yancy. "Get me a blanket off the top of the coach for Miss Bangs."

Yancy complied swiftly. Gunn stretched Hortense's body out, folding her hands across her stomach. Her eyes were closed. She looked at peace. When Yancy brought the blanket, Gunn stretched it over her. He climbed out of the coach. The women looked at him questioningly.

"Hallman's O.K. He'll be around, I reckon."

"What about Miss Bangs?" asked Janice.

"She's laid out as best as could be."

Gunn turned to Yancy.

115

"You can help me cut this team loose, and put bridles on 'em."

"Can I talk to you a moment?"

"Sure."

"Private."

Yancy held something in his hands. A leather pouch. A bullet had ripped it open. Papers showed through. Yancy clutched it as if it were made of gold.

Gunn walked to the back of the coach, around the other side. He spoke to Esquire, who stood there hipshot. Yancy followed. They were out of sight of the women.

"Look at what I found up there," said Yancy. "The papers had come out and I was putting them back in when I saw this."

He extracted a document and handed it to Gunn. Gunn read it. His jaw hardened.

"It's enough to hang him," he said.

"I know. What should we do?"

"Nothing. I'll keep this. Put that pouch back and don't let him know you found it."

"It was right there by the medicine bag. I didn't mean to pry."

"You did fine, Yancy. If he knows you've seen this, though, he'll kill you."

"Damn. I thought he was a fine man. He said you were an outlaw."

Gunn patted Yancy on the back, and stuck the paper in his belt. It was a letter and it explained everything—the rifles, the Apaches, even Captain Rice. He wondered that Hallman hadn't kept the document on his person. Or burned it. He didn't know yet how to make use of it, but he'd have to see to it that it got into the proper hands. The trouble was, he was an outlaw. That is, he was accused of a crime he didn't commit and there was a bounty on his head. That made it hard for him to approach anyone in authority, especially a United States Marshal or an army captain.

He saddled up the strongest team horse, and put bridles on the others. Luckily, Ned had kept a good tack. There was another saddle in the boot. He put that on another horse.

"What are we going to do?" asked Janice.

"Ride to Tucson," said Gunn.

"What about Mr. Hallman?"

"He'll have to make it on his own."

"You mean you're just going to leave him here?"

"Yes. He'd slow us down. He's got medicine. He can doctor himself. He can ride the other horse with a saddle. Miss Heller can ride with me and you can ride with Yancy. I'll be pulling my horse."

Amity smiled when he said this.

"I've never ridden a horse," said Yancy.

"About time you learned."

"I'll ride, you sit behind me," said Janice.

"What about all our things? My clothes?" asked Amity.

"Leave them," said Gunn. "We'll send a wagon back from Dragoon Springs if there's anyone there."

There was a commotion inside the coach.

Hallman stepped out, a pistol in his hand. He was reeling, trying hard not to fall.

"You seem to be in an all-fired hurry, Gunn," he said.

Gunn looked at the pistol in Hallman's hands.

It steadied, coming to rest level with his belt buckle.

"I have my reasons."

"And you would just ride off and leave me?"

"I reckon you know where to go, Hallman. These women have to get to a place of safety and shelter. The Apaches might come back."

"They might. And what chance would I have?"

"Why don't you ask Sangre? Or Jennings?"

Hallman's mouth twisted to a savage snarl. He cocked the pistol.

Gunn didn't wait.

He went into a crouch, slashing his hand downward to his Colt. Janice screamed. Amity reached out, grabbed his left arm. Gunn jerked his pistol free, cocking it as he brought it level.

Hallman took aim, like a gentleman lining up for a duel.

"Don't kill him!" yelled Janice, from a few yards away. "Gunn, don't!"

CHAPTER ELEVEN

Gunn measured his life in seconds.

His life and Hallman's were on the line. The ex-army man stood no more than ten paces away, his Remington aimed straight at Gunn's head. Hallman was good. With any other man he might have been victorious. Most men did not aim and shoot. They fired their pistols before they were half ready. When the pressure was on, they fired them into the ground, or up in the air. Or off to the side. It took a lot of courage to shoot a man. Courage or hatred. When it came to a showdown, most men could not aim dead center and pull the trigger when the target was another human being.

But Hallman was army. He had probably fought duels. He had studied the rules. His training had taught him a certain method and that was his undoing. Gunn did not live by the rules. Not Hallman's rules. He lived by a code of survival that had been honed since that day up on the Cache de la Poudre when he vowed to kill the man who had raped and murdered his wife.

He heard Janice plead with him not to shoot Hallman, but Janice's life wasn't on the line.

It was too late, anyway.

Hallman was taking dead aim.

Gunn's finger tightened on the trigger.

The Colt .45 felt snug and easy in his hand. Another second and a life would be ended. It was so easy. So hard. A man shouldn't die so easy. Not without a chance to reason with his enemy. Hallman had called it. Hallman had thrown down on him.

But did that make any difference?

Maybe.

Hallman would kill him if he didn't defend himself.

The trouble was, when anger reached the flash point, there was no reasoning anymore. Once a man pulled the trigger, he could not stop the firing pin from falling on the primer. Once the powder ignited, he could not stop the bullet.

Once a man was dead, nothing could bring him back to life.

Once a trigger was pulled, the death process was set in motion.

"Gunn!"

Yancy's voice was followed by the metallic click of a shell sliding into the breech of a Spencer carbine.

Gunn's finger froze on the trigger.

"Mr. Hallman," said Yancy, "you hold it right there. If you make another move I'll shoot you."

Gunn turned his head slightly, looking at the youth.

Meredith Yancy had the rifle up to his shoulder. His neck was slightly bent. He was aiming. His finger was on the trigger of the Spencer. The barrel swung slowly from man to man. From Gunn to Hallman.

"Easy, kid," said Hallman.

"Don't call me kid, sir. I mean what I say. This is stupid. All of it. You want to kill Gunn and he will surely kill you first. I'll do anything I can to stop it."

"You'd kill, too," said Hallman, lowering his pistol. "Wouldn't you?"

"I—I don't know. I just can't watch this happen. It's wrong."

Gunn stood up from his crouch and covered his hammer with his palm. It had been close. Very close.

Yancy was still holding the rifle steady, still aiming. At Gunn.

"Please, Meredith. Don't do anything foolish," said Janice.

"Put your pistols away, sirs," said Yancy.

Hallman stretched out his arm to steady himself against the Concord. He twisted the pistol around and shoved it into his holster, butt out. Gunn eased the hammer down on the Colt and holstered it. Yancy lowered the barrel of the carbine.

Amity and Janice let out twin sighs of relief.

"I'll take one of those horses," said Hallman.

"Go ahead," said Gunn, stepping aside. "But if I see you again, Hallman, it'll be too soon."

Hallman said something to Yancy. The youth climbed atop the coach, and threw down a valise and the pouch. Hallman put on a fresh shirt and a coat, and tucked the pouch inside a pocket without examining it. Gunn watched him carefully. He mounted up, and rode off toward Dragoon Springs.

"Where is he going?" asked Yancy.

"I wish I knew," said Gunn. "But you can bet there'll be trouble later on."

"I couldn't just let you shoot him. Kill him. You would have killed him, wouldn't you? I mean, you would have beat him to it."

"I reckon," said Gunn.

He looked up at the sullen sky, at the gnarled growth of the land that was jumbled with rocks. The Apaches had been well organized. There were not many of them, but they had done their job smoothly. They had ten or twelve braves waiting in the rocks, and another six or

121

eight on ponies. They had killed Wales deliberately, but had not been interested in the others. And, from what he had heard them say, in Spanish, Hallman's wound was an accident. They had not meant to kill him. He wondered how Captain Rice fit into all this. Hallman had a story about that, but it was not necessarily the right one. The papers he had in his pocket sent a chill up Gunn's spine. The enormity of Hallman's scheme made him shudder.

And, the horror was, it might work.

Gunn wished there had been one more bridle. Given time, he could have rigged a rope halter, but maybe it was best to keep everyone together. He loaded Esquire lightly, with water bags and spare ammunition. He carried his own bedroll behind his saddle, and ammunition for his Winchester and Colt in his saddlebags. Satisfied that they had packed all that they could, he ordered Janice, Amity, and Yancy to mount up.

"I just want you to know I think you're trash, Gunn," said Amity, pouting with defiance. "The way you treated Mr. Hallman. He was right about you. You're a cold-blooded killer."

"Yes'm," said Gunn. "Now get your ass up on that horse before I kick it up there."

Amity gasped.

"I—I wouldn't ride with you if you were the last man on earth."

"You can ride with me, Miss Heller," said Yancy, ever the polite young man.

"Do you have any objection to riding behind me, Miss Longworth?" asked Gunn.

"I don't suppose I have any choice, do I?"

"You can walk," said Gunn.

"I could ride with Amity and you and Mr. Yancy could go together."

"And if we get separated?"

Janice stamped her foot in frustration. She hiked up her skirts and walked over to the horse. She swung up into the saddle easily, carrying the Spencer. Gunn mounted right behind her. She sat behind the cantle.

"How do I hold on?" she asked.

"Either by my belt, or put your arm around my waist."

Begrudgingly, Janice wrapped an arm around Gunn's waist and grabbed his belt. He grinned to himself, watching as Yancy and Amity struggled to get on the bareback horse. Finally, Amity had to help Yancy stay on. She rode in front, sitting up straight, giving Gunn another defiant glance.

"Lead on, Miss Heller," said Gunn. "Just follow the road down."

The horse balked, and Gunn rode up and slapped its rump. It bolted into a jarring trot.

Janice laughed.

"They look funny," she said.

"I'm glad to see you have a sense of humor," said Gunn.

"Wait'll I tell the authorities about you, Gunn. Let's see if you still like my sense of humor then."

Gunn said nothing. He tied Esquire's rope to a saddle ring, and touched rowelless spurs to the horse's flanks. The horse moved out in an easy lope under the leaden sky.

Smoke signals followed them almost all the way to Dragoon Springs. From way back in the hills, white puffs dotted the sky. Answering puffs came from miles away. Gunn wished that he could understand them. He

123

now knew that Sangre's braves were all along the old stage road. In the pass, they had been hit by a small band. Sangre was evidently confident enough to send those few to get the Spencers off the coach.

But that wasn't all. Something was brewing. The Apaches didn't use smoke just to tell of the white people riding toward the Springs. There had to be something big afoot. Hallman's letter explained some of it. When they got to Tucson, he was going to have to trust someone. Yancy, or one of the women. And right now, he was sure the ladies would probably think he had forged the document he carried himself.

The monotonous plains were skirted with high hills. Dusk was approaching by the time Gunn and the others reached the Springs. The women were irritable and Yancy seemed dejected at having to ride behind Amity.

"We can't go on," said Amity. "I ache all over."

"We ought to go on," said Gunn. He, too, was weary.

"Let's vote on it," said Yancy.

Gunn surveyed the crumbling adobes, the rotting corrals. It was a good enough place to stay. Likely, the Apaches had gone on west. Had they wanted to kill them, they would have done it back at the pass. It was light enough to see and he went over the ground carefully. Hallman had passed this way, and gone on to the San Pedro Valley. There were other tracks, too, from shod horses and three or four unshod ponies. From the signs, he guessed that Jennings and Kelly had waited here. There were cigarette butts and a recently emptied bottle of mezcal. The tracks told him a lot, but they raised even more questions.

He wondered, for instance, why the Apaches had attacked the stage and taken the rifles at that place? Why hadn't they waited for Hallman to deliver them? For Gunn was now certain that the Spencers were never destined for Rice. That was just a smoke screen that Hallman had created. And why had Jennings waited here?

The hills were crawling with Apaches. The trail was virtually deserted.

Gunn felt the hackles crawling on the back of his neck. Something was going on that he didn't know about and it was not good. The only explanation was that the Apaches needed those Spencers before they were due to be delivered by Hallman. Either the soldiers were pursuing them or they were already on the blood trail mentioned in the letter to Hallman that Gunn had in his pocket.

"Are we going to stay here?"

So absorbed in his thoughts was Gunn that he had not heard Janice walk up behind him. He was staring at a column of smoke that was different from the signals they had seen all afternoon.

"We can," said Gunn. "Maybe we'd better."

Janice saw the smoke, too.

"What's that?"

"I don't know. But there used to be a ranch over that way. Owned by a man named St. John."

"I don't understand."

"Neither do I, but I haven't seen any smoke signals for the last two hours and that's a fresh blaze. Look at the way the smoke boils up. If you look hard, you can see flames underneath."

Janice looked. The sun was down, but the afterglow lingered in the sky. "Yes," she said excitedly, "I see it now. There is a fire!"

Amity and Yancy heard the loud talk and came over, leading the horses.

"What's going on?" asked Yancy. Then he saw the huge funnel of smoke spewing into the paint-daubed sky. The black smoke was darker than the low gray clouds that had turned all colors with the setting of the sun.

"Gunn says that there might be a ranch there," said Janice. "Owned by a man named St. John. Do you know him, Gunn?"

"I know of him. Everyone does. He almost lost his life at this very spot."

"Here?" asked Amity.

"Tell you at supper," said Gunn. "Let's get the horses settled and a fire started."

"I'm surprised at you," said Janice, looking at Gunn. He sat a few feet away from her, his gray eyes flickering with firelight. "With just a few pans and the food in your saddlebags, you made a good supper."

"I'm no cook."

"You saved us with that meal."

Gunn had made it quick: beef, bacon, and shortcake. Easy to fix. More elaborate than he would have made for himself. Like a lot of men, he could cook, but he would probably have starved if he had to do it only for himself. He had brought enough supplies in his saddlebags to get them by until they hit Tucson. Janice, and the others, would tire of such fare if they had a month of it. The ride had made them all hungry. They would have eaten buffalo chips if it was fixed right.

Amity looked at Gunn through eyelash-shielded eyes.

"It was good. And filling. Thank you, Gunn. I was famished."

"You did it so fast," said Yancy, marveling. "I didn't even think about how we would eat."

"Out here," said Gunn, "there's no grocer. You have to worry about your belly so your mind stays quick."

"You're a strange man," said Amity. "I mean you

seem more at home here. I can't picture you anywhere else."

Had she softened?

Gunn looked at her, thought of how she had been the night before. Women puzzled him. They were so sure at times, so vulnerable at others. Amity was a child, really, but at times she seemed very wise.

"The way to live is to be at home wherever you are. I've liked all the places I've been. I carry them with me."

"Like a home," said Janice, suddenly thoughtful.

"You make your home where you can," said Gunn.

Yancy rattled the stained coffee pot on the rocks of the fire circle. The pot hissed; steam poured from its spout.

"It boiled," he said. "Smells strong."

"Pour it," said Gunn, nodding to the ladies. "It'll be chill tonight."

The fire glow in the sky over at St. John's place had died down, darkening the night. The clouds hid the stars, the moon.

Yancy poured coffee into two cups. He and Gunn would have to share, as would the ladies.

"What were you going to tell us about St. John?" asked Janice.

Gunn let Yancy take the first drink of coffee, then took the cup. He blew on it, scattering steam.

"I don't remember all the details," said Gunn, "but the story was told along many trails. It happened back in '58 when John Butterfield was just setting up a station here. About August, the company's road construction gang left Silas St. John, who was from New York, in charge of six men to complete the work on this station. The men were James Hughes of Watertown, New York, James Laing of Kentucky, William Cunningham of Iowa, and three Mexican laborers, Guadalupe Ramirez, Pablo Ramirez, both of

Sonora, and Bonifacio Mirando of Chihuahua. They called Pablo, 'Chino,' because of his oriental features.

"Early in September, St. John changed the guard, posting Guadalupe in Laing's place. About one o'clock in the morning, the Mexicans grabbed axes and attacked Hughes. They killed him right off. Then they jumped on Laing and Cunningham, wounding them both. They hacked up St. John's arm. He fought back, firing his pistol with his good hand, and drove the Mexicans off."

Gunn paused, handing his coffee to Yancy.

"How horrible!" exclaimed Amity.

"I remember reading about that," said Yancy. "A feller named Waterman Ormbsy wrote about it in the *New York Herald.*"

"What happened then?" asked Janice, utterly fascinated by the story. Gunn looked into the flickering fire and pulled out his makings. He began rolling a cigarette as he continued the story.

"Well, Cunningham died the following night. Laing was badly wounded and delirious, but he hung on. So did St. John, who had lost a lot of blood and had a badly mangled arm. They kept thinking the Mexicans might come back to finish them off, but St. John's pistol had proved more than they bargained for. Nobody came until the celerity wagon with the road crew got back on Sunday. Col. James Leach was on his way back to California with the crew. The next night, Monday, Laing died. St. John was in poor shape. The assistant post surgeon, B.J.D. Irwin didn't get in from Fort Buchanan until Friday morning. He amputated St. John's arm. Six days later he was moved to the fort where he stayed for about three weeks. Then he mounted a horse and rode to Tucson. Later, he built that ranch. He's still looking for those Mexicans, I hear, and if the Apaches haven't killed him, he might find them yet."

"That would be terrible if he should die after surviving that ordeal," said Janice.

"Not many men could live for four days and three nights with those wounds," said Gunn. "He was so weak he couldn't get food or water, either. He has a strong heart."

"Why did the Mexicans try to kill them?" asked Amity.

"Money. They stole some money and made off with it. It was pretty lonesome out here then. Men get funny ideas."

"It's lonesome out here now," said Yancy. "Do you think we ought to ride on in the dark? I'm some spooked after listening to that story."

Gunn chuckled, blew smoke into the air.

"We should go on. The Apaches will be busy bragging about what they did this day and we won't have to worry about them tonight."

"I wonder why they didn't kill us all today?" asked Janice.

"Hard telling," said Gunn.

"But you think you know why, don't you?"

"I've wondered about it myself. They could have killed us men and taken you two ladies with them. I would have understood that."

"But they didn't," said Amity quickly. "Maybe they just wanted the rifles."

"Oh, they want the rifles all right. But these Apaches are wild, desperate. Taking a couple of white women with them wouldn't have made much difference to them."

Yancy started poking at the fire with a stick. A shower of sparks rose up in the air.

"Why don't you tell them about the letter, Gunn?"

"Think they'd believe me?"

"What letter?" asked Janice, leaning forward after batting away a few sparks.

"Yes, what letter?" chorused Amity.

"Well, let's say a man wanted a lot of land cheap. And he had some backers who wanted to run cattle on a large spread. Texas was too expensive and too crowded, but there was all this space. And yet, there were already ranches taking up the good water. What better way to get the Americans off and lower the price of land than to finance an Apache uprising."

"Are you saying Mr. Hallman was doing such a thing?" asked Amity.

"I have a letter here that says that much. And Jennings is helping him. You asked why you weren't captured and all of us killed? I think I have an answer."

"Please tell us, then, and I want to see that letter for myself," said Janice, her skepticism showing on her face.

"I'll show you the letter, surely. And you'll have to take my hunch on blind faith."

"All right," she said, still unconvinced.

"I think," said Gunn, "that Hallman wanted Ned Wales killed. But I also think he wanted witnesses so that he would be in the clear. You and Amity and young Yancy here would be perfect."

"What about Miss Bangs?"

"Funny thing about that," said Gunn, tossing his cigarette butt into the fire. "She was shot at close range. With a .44. Pistol round, I'd say. Hallman didn't want her alive. He didn't want Wales alive. Or me. But you three would be all right. He's older than you and he could sway your opinion."

"I don't believe any of this for one minute," said Amity.

"Nor do I," said Janice. "Do you have any proof?"

"Maybe," Gunn said, his voice low, his gray eyes

flickering in the light. "When I dressed Hallman's wound I noticed there were powder burns all around it. And he was shot with a .44 too."

"So?" asked Yancy, eagerly following Gunn's train of thought.

"Hallman packs a .44 Remington and I heard the Apaches talking Spanish. They said he was to be left alive."

CHAPTER TWELVE

Jacob Hallman sipped from the bottle of laudanum. His shoulder wound throbbed. He cursed his mistake. He meant only to give himself a superficial flesh wound in the shoulder after killing Hortense Bangs. But the coach had taken a lurch when his finger was pulling the trigger. The ball had gone into the muscle. Now the wound throbbed. The alcohol and opium distillate helped, but he was groggy from riding hard.

He followed the smoke signs and rendezvoused with Sangre an hour out of Dragoon Springs. Wearily, he dismounted from his horse and sagged onto a rock. The camp was atop a hill with a view all around. Far below, he could see the buildings of St. John's ranch.

Jennings and Kelly were there, too.

"Expected you sooner," said Jennings. "That's what the smoke said."

"I got winged in the shoot out. Every mile jarred the wound."

A brave was just smothering the fire. Apaches sat on rocks and leaned against scrub pines or junipers, playing with the new Spencers. Sangre, drinking from an earthen *olla,* grinned at Hallman.

"You and me have two good arms between us,

Jay Cobb."

"Why in hell didn't your braves kill that sonofa-bitchin' Gunn?"

"They say he have much medicine."

Jacob Hallman grunted in disgust. Things were not going well. But at least the Apaches had the rifles.

"You ready to hit St. John?" he asked Sangre.

"When it is almost dark."

"Good. I want him burned out. He's a hero around here. When word gets to Tucson, you'll be able to sweep to the Gila."

"You give back all the land to the Apache, huh?" asked Sangre.

Hallman knew he had to be careful with Sangre. He was not only a smart Injun, but he could smell bullshit a mile away. He knew the white man's tongue and he was an outlaw, a renegade, even among his own kind. Besides that, Sangre was dangerous, unpredictable.

"Sangre, you must learn patience. *Paciencia*. There will be land for you and for your people. You must defend it, as I must defend what I gain here."

"You are *muy sabio*. I know. Very smart *hombre*. You say you know way to keep soldier out of Apache land. You tell Sangre how soldier no hunt Apache."

Hallman sighed wearily. He did not fool the Apache chief.

"Even as we talk, Sangre, Maj. Jamison Heller is riding for Tucson. He will arrest Captain Rice, the soldier who hunts you, and court-martial him. Rice will go to the white man's prison. Savvy? And Major Heller will be glad to have his daughter safe. He will ride back to the Presidio at San Francisco in the white man's state of California. There will be no soldiers from Fort Yuma to El Paso. There will be no white men except my friends and me. We will run many cattle and you will share. You will eat for as long as the sun shines

133

and the rivers flow."

"How you do this?"

Hallman patted the document pouch in his inside jacket pocket. Except that the pouch was not there. His face blanched as he realized that he had left it atop the stage. His stomach twisted, churned. Beads of sweat broke out on his forehead.

"You sick?"

"No. I just forgot something, that's all. It's not important."

Sangre stood up, favoring his wounded shoulder. He was a small man, wiry, and yet the paint on his swarthy face made him appear tall, fierce. He made a sign to his lounging braves. He made the circle for the sun and let his hand fall gracefully to the backside of his other hand. He forked two fingers and straddled the index finger of his left hand. His hands moved like birds telling his followers to make ready to attack the rancho below the peak.

Jennings watched Sangre and spoke in whispering tones to Kelly.

"Too bad we can't wait around for the fun," he said.

"Where we going?" asked Kelly.

"Tucson. Hallman's meeting Heller there."

"Jesus. He plans like a goddamned general."

Jennings nodded. His eyes widened, filled with a light like fox fire on the marshes. It was a light like greed.

Hallman was a planner. He made few mistakes. Like the breed. Hallman had been suspicious of the man from the first. Hallman carried a little tin mirror in his coat. He had flashed the word about Choya. The last person in the world Jennings would suspect, him being Sangre's half nephew and all. But Choya had been in with Ben Aquilar, apparently.

"How'd you find out about Choya?" Jennings

134

asked Hallman.

"He was too good to be true. Found out he had worked as a scout for the army, knew Jon Rice. He was soft. I think he would have reported to Rice once we got to Tucson."

"Likely. Sangre, he didn't bat an eye about him."

"No. Sangre doesn't like mixed bloods."

"He don't like nothin' much. Tough bastard."

Hallman got up, wincing as his shoulder moved. It was time to go on to Tucson to spread the word about the attack.

"Let's ride. We don't want to be around here when Sangre hits that rancho."

"We're ready," said Jennings. "Kelly, fetch up our horses."

Kelly's nose twitched.

"Be glad to get away from the smell of these Injuns," he said in a low voice. "They stink to high heaven."

"Watch you don't let Sangre hear you," said Jennings.

"Fuck Sangre."

Hallman frowned. He needed Kelly for a while, but he wouldn't grieve any if he was out of the way. Kelly talked too much and he was lazy besides. Jennings now, was a different matter. He fed on hate. He did what he was told and he did it well. Kelly was Jennings's man, but he was about to outlive his usefulness. There was no way of telling how far Sangre was willing to go. With the Spencers he had a chance, but if Rice caught up with him at the wrong time, Sangre would just disappear into the hills.

And that wouldn't do. Not just yet.

Gunn watched the fire die.

He was restless, but the women had told him they

135

were too tired to go on that night. Yancy had voted with them.

There were not enough blankets to go around. Janice and Amity had made a bed and were sleeping together. He and Yancy would have to stay warm as best they could.

"Time to move this fire," said Gunn. "Ground's warm, but it won't last."

Yancy yawned. He had been half asleep.

Sticks and brush had been stacked some distance away. Now, Gunn and Yancy pushed the coals from the first fire toward the dry tinder. They swept the coals before them with brush. The tinder caught. Gunn swept the place where the old fire had been to make sure there were no small coals left.

"I'll take the first watch, Yancy."

"My name's Meredith."

"That what they called you back East?"

Yancy flushed.

"They called me 'Merry.'"

"That's no name for a man."

"I know. You don't think much of me, do you?"

Gunn looked at him. Yancy was young, but he was learning. He could grow out here. If he kept his eyes open and his back straight.

"You'll do," he said.

"Gunn, I haven't done much with my life. I haven't earned any money on my own. My folks left me some and now my uncle's died and left me some more. I came out here to—to—"

"To what?"

"I—I don't know. I guess I just got tired of people looking down at me, calling me a wastrel and a ne'er-do-well. I tried to make my own way but I just kept meeting people who wanted to skin me out of my money."

"Money can be a problem," admitted Gunn. "Especially easy money."

"My pa was a storekeeper. He began buying for other stores and then opened a manufacturing plant. He made some good investments. He and my ma were looking at a powder plant. It blew up and killed them both."

"Tough."

"He always told me to come West."

"What happened to his businesses?"

"I found out he had partners. They bought me out. I didn't even have a job after Pa died. Just the money."

"You have to live with it."

"I know. I just want to do it my own way. A lot of people came to me with schemes, business propositions. None of them were any good."

Gunn hefted the Winchester.

"You get some rest, Yance—Meredith. I'll take a turn around the camp."

Yancy smiled wanly.

"Thanks for listening to me."

"My pleasure," said Gunn.

The young man lay on the spot warmed by the previous fire. He wadded up his hat for a pillow. The women were inside one of the adobes, out of the wind if it rose during the night. The clouds broke up an hour or so later and the stars came into view. The moon, half full, dusted the land with a muted silver.

Gunn walked a wide circle well out of the firelight. His eyes quickly adjusted to the dark. A rabbit scurried nearby and stopped, blinking until he coughed. It hopped away. A coyote yapped on a low hill two miles away, sounding close. An owl floated by on silent wings, hunting.

The fiery glow in the sky finally diminished. Gunn

wondered if St. John had escaped death a second time.

"Amity? Are you still awake?"

"Umm."

"What do you think of Gunn? Do you believe him?"

"I don't know, Janice. Do you?"

"I—I'm not sure. When I look into those pale blue eyes of his he seems so honest. But Mr. Hallman is respected. He was in the army."

"So was Gunn," said Amity.

Their voices were low, whispery. Their bodies touching under the blankets kept them warm. They could see the stars through the rotted sod roof of the adobe.

"I didn't know that."

"Miss Bangs said that Mulejaw told her that. He was a hero. At a place called Missionary Ridge."

"I still don't know what to think. Do you believe Mr. Hallman killed Miss Bangs and shot himself?"

"I was so scared with all that yelling and shooting. I can't believe Mr. Hallman would just shoot her. And then himself."

"Me neither. I think Gunn just wants to believe that. He doesn't like Hallman and he's probably afraid of going to prison for murder."

"Don't talk that way, Janice. You're scaring me. To think of a murderer walking around like that."

There was a long pause. Amity closed her eyes and turned over. Janice pulled the blankets back over her.

"I think I killed an Indian today," said Janice. "Does that make me a murderer?"

"No, silly. You were defending yourself."

"I was scared too."

"Go to sleep, Janice. I ache all over from being on

that horse."

"Good night, Amity."

"Good night, Janice."

But Janice couldn't sleep. She, too, was tired and her muscles ached. Her mind drifted to the puzzle that was Gunn. He was attractive. Miss Bangs had slept with him. Amity had flirted with him. So had she. She wondered if it was because he was unlike any man she'd ever met that she was interested in him. Or if she was just fascinated at knowing a man who was a wanted murderer.

She finally drifted off to sleep, the puzzle no nearer solution than before. The only thing she knew was that she wanted to know more about Gunn. She wanted, if possible, to know the truth about the man. And, perhaps, she wanted to know him in a primitive, earthy way, a way that made her shiver with longing when she turned over and lay nestled against Amity under the blankets.

The Apaches skulked through the hills, setting up positions around the St. John ranch. They built fires and set torches. They threw the torches onto the buildings. The ranch was ablaze before any of the white settlers knew they were under attack. The Apaches shot the defenders who tried to put out the fires. St. John escaped without being wounded because he had been tending a sick cow some three miles from the house when the Apaches began shooting. He rode up, saw that he would lose everything, and turned his horse without looking back.

He rode straight for Tucson.

This was not Silas St. John, but his son, Seth. Silas was in Tucson on business.

Seth was a strapping youth who had first-hand

experience with Indians. He knew the difference between a Mescalero and a Mimbreno, a Chiricahua and a Yaqui. Those who had attacked the rancho were Mescaleros and, by the markings on their arms, were part of Sangre's band.

He had been expecting such a raid, but not that day. Not that day particularly. They had seen the smoke signals and knew something was brewing. He had told his men to arm themselves and be careful. Then, the rains had come, swelling the creeks, causing flash floods. Cattle had been caught in the torrent, injured, scattered. All day they'd been out chasing down strays, counting the drowned animals. The rest of the men had gone back and he had stayed to help a half-drowned yearling that had been smashed against some rocks. The animal was on its feet and might survive. He was grateful to that brindle longhorn. It had saved his life. He knew that those at the ranch had been killed, slaughtered without a chance.

The Mescaleros must have struck swiftly, without warning. He had counted more than a dozen and heard that many more yelling and screaming for blood.

Seth rode hard to Tucson through the night, crossing the Cienega at flood tide, whipping his horse through the swollen waters at the ford. He hated to bring bad news to his father, who had survived a murderous attempt on his life more than a dozen years before, but it had to be done. Besides, he had heard that the army was in Tucson now, hunting renegade Apaches. Even though the ranch would probably be lost, they could rebuild. If his father had the heart for it.

Seth was thirteen years old and he had been spawned in the rough land over which he rode. He hated Apaches more than anything on earth.

An Apache had killed his mother five years before. Not in a raid, but in town. The Indian was drunk, shooting off his pistol. The bullet had struck his mother in the arm, and had gone through to her heart. She had died on the street in Tucson with Seth crying for her to wake up, to hold him, to stop bleeding.

Seth St. John arrived in Tucson shortly after dawn.

Jacob Hallman, Kelly, and Jennings had ridden in a short time before.

Seth's timing could not have been better for Hallman's purposes. A crowd had already gathered at the Tecolote Saloon when young St. John came riding in, his horse lathered to a froth, his face smeared with dust and sweat.

"We were hit in Apache Pass," said Hallman to the assemblage, "without warning. They were vicious as a pack of wild dogs. Ned Wales was killed and a young pretty woman. I was run off from helping by a wanted outlaw. A man named Gunn."

The crowd listened to the news and murmured their outrage as Hallman laid it on thick as butter slabs.

"Repeating rifles were stolen by the Injuns and that means one thing. The Mescaleros are on the warpath."

The crowd jostled, and moved closer.

"I wanted to go after them, though sorely wounded, but this Gunn drove me off at gunpoint. There's a thousand dollar reward on his head. If he comes to Tucson, beware. He's mean and he's no count. And, he's got two young women with him, one of whom he's already violated."

The crowd of men and women turned surly. Angry voices interlocked in a furious exchange.

Hallman stood on the steps of the porch looking at each one in turn. The rider came up to the edge and stopped, listening.

"I don't know if Gunn is in cahoots with the

Apaches, but he's a treacherous man and I'd bet my last dollar that he's in with Sangre."

Seth St. John heard Hallman's words and waved his hat in the air for attention.

"We were burned out by the Mescaleros last night," he croaked. "All my father's men were killed. My friends. Nobody had a chance. Two dozen of 'em, at least, and screamin'. My knees was jelly. My stomach turned over a hundred times so afeard was I and the fire eatin' up all my pa built. The Apaches had repeating rifles. We didn't have a chance. What this man says is true. I'm on my way to the St. John to see my pa and tell him what happened."

"You be Seth, Silas's boy," said a bystander.

"I am, and my horse is plumb wore out from runnin' all night."

Voices rose up.

"Get the boy's horse to the livery."

"Take him over to Silas's."

Hallman waved his arms for attention.

"Folks, you can see I spoke the truth. The Apaches are wearing paint and they've got repeaters. You'd better arm yourselves and expect the worst."

A young man stepped forward.

"Mister, we got cavalry in town."

Hallman's face paled slightly. He fought to compose himself.

"Army?"

"Yes sir. Cap'n Rice come in last night. He's bivouacked at the end of Main Street. Fact is, he's bunked at St. John's hotel."

"Why that's good news," said Hallman. "I'll meet with him. I'm a friend of his."

"We ought to go in and have a drink," said a man at the back of the crowd. "Get ourselves organized."

Seth St. John slid from his saddle, and let men take

his horse. He was barely able to stand and two men helped him down the street, toward his father's hotel.

Jennings, standing on the porch, came near Hallman and spoke to him.

"Looks like you got 'em stirred up right proper," he said.

"Yeah," said Hallman. "Now I have to convince Jon Rice that Gunn was in on this."

"The stolen rifles? How do you figger that?"

"Hell, easy. Rice is a friend of mine. He'll believe anything I tell him."

"What about those Spencers? He's gonna wanta know where they came from."

"Oh he knows I bought 'em. But he thinks I was going to sell them to the ranchers along the Gila."

"Christ, Jake, you don't miss a danged trick."

Kelly moved up from the back of the porch. People streamed up the steps, knocking aside the batwing doors of the Tecolote.

"Looks as though you don't have to go lookin' for Rice," said Kelly. "Here he comes now."

Hallman and Jennings looked up the street.

Capt. Jonathan Rice and a lieutenant, a sergeant, and corporal were riding in formation right for the Tecolote.

"See?" said Hallman. "Everything works."

"Huh?" asked Jennings.

"Rice is going to look at this hole in my shoulder and believe every damn word I tell him."

Hallman turned away, bent over. He took out the bottle of laudanum and took a deep swig. His eyes swam, but his stomach blossomed with a friendly heat.

Everything was turning out fine.

Everything worked.

CHAPTER THIRTEEN

The cougar coughed.

Gunn, half dozing, heard the sound and stiffened. He jerked his shoulder away from the rock and shook his head to clear it of sleepiness.

He must have dozed off, he thought. The stars tilted as he looked up at them. Below, he saw the bare outlines of the adobe where the young women were sleeping. The sound had come from that direction.

He could almost smell the big cat.

That cough was unmistakable.

Dry, low in the throat, fetid with stale air.

He was upwind, so the animal hadn't scented him. The cougar must have slipped up from the rimrocks below the station and padded up to the abandoned clearing after game.

Gunn waited, listening.

The cougar grunted again and Gunn could almost see its chest sag and then take in air.

He stalked down the slope, toward the adobe.

Picking his way carefully, Gunn hunched over. The cougar was too close to the women. Someone could get hurt. The fire had burned low and he realized he must have dozed off longer than he thought. He had replenished it once with greasewood and mesquite that had taken him the better part of an hour to gather. Yancy had been fast asleep when he had put the fresh fuel on the fire.

The cougar coughed again.

Maybe this was its territory and it resented the intrusion. Maybe it was just curious. Cougars did not hunt humans. Not unless there was something wrong with the big cats. If they were old, toothless, they would sometimes attack a human. Or, if they were hurt and cornered, sometimes they would jump on a man and bite him.

The danger here was that the cougar might go inside the adobe and scare the women. Unless it got out fast, and felt safe, it might lash out and do some clawing. It was pitch-dark and he couldn't see a thing. The shadows around the adobe were deep. He tried to mark the last place he had heard the cougar. Directly below him. Smack dab where the adobe loomed in the dark.

Suddenly, a scream tore through the night air.

A woman's scream.

Then, Gunn heard the snarl of the cat.

Another scream, this one high pitched, full of stark terror.

Gunn raced headlong down the slope, jacking a shell into the chamber of the Winchester.

The snarls and screams came from within the adobe. In the dark, Gunn searched for the opening. Part of a wall had collapsed, sealing off the back door. He raced around to the front. The screams were now short, staccato, both women's voices mingling in a blood-curdling cacophony.

"Shut up!" yelled Gunn, racing around the corner.

The screams rose in pitch and intensity. He realized the horses were screaming too, snorting and pawing, trying to break their reins. He hoped the leather would hold. Horses were terrified of cougars.

He heard the cat spit and hiss. It coughed and growled, evidently cornered with the two hysterical women.

"Don't move!" said Gunn.

He heard pounding footfalls, turned, saw a shape running toward him.

"Yancy! Stay out of the way!"

Gunn went inside the adobe, bent to a half crouch.

In the faint light from the stars, he saw the white-clad women frozen in a corner. The cat was only a tawny shadow sitting in the center of the room, batting a single paw in the air.

The cougar turned, a mass of muscles, sinews, claws, and fangs, its hide rippling with power. It hunkered down and prepared to leap straight at Gunn. He couldn't fire. If he missed, the bullet might strike one of the girls. Their screams intensified and the big cat spooked.

With a snarl, the cougar raced two steps and took to the air. It came at Gunn, claws extended, jaws open wide, fangs glistening a dull white in the darkness.

Gunn dropped to the earthen floor, bringing the rifle up defensively. As the cat struck, he swiped upward, then rolled away. The butt smashed into the cougar's jaw. Claws raked his clothing. Snarling and spitting, the cat landed off balance. It twisted, lashing out with a lethal paw. Gunn felt the rush of air past his face. He brought the rifle up, rammed the snout into the animal's side. He pulled the trigger.

The smell of black powder permeated the adobe. The cat screamed in pain and rolled over, clawing at its side. Gunn scrambled to his feet and levered another shell into the chamber. The cat tumbled toward the door, away from the women. Gunn stepped up to it, fired another shot point-blank. The cat shook and lay still, its lungs and heart shattered by the .44 slug.

"It's all right," said Gunn. "You can stop screaming."

"Is it—dead?" sniffled Amity.

"Yes."

"Get it out of here," she whimpered.

"Meredith!" Gunn called. "Lend a hand."

Yancy came running up, out of breath. The cougar lay sprawled in the doorway. He hesitated.

"Grab its front legs," said Gunn.

"It's huge," said the young man in a single expulsion of breath.

"Big enough."

They hefted the cougar and lugged it some distance away from the crumbling adobe.

The women ventured out, swaddled in blankets. Janice came up to Gunn and stood close to him, looking down at the dead shape on the ground.

"You saved our lives," she breathed.

"Cat was more scared of you than you were of it," he said.

"Oh no," said Amity. "I've never been so scared in my life."

Yancy laughed. Then Amity joined in. Janice chuckled, but moved close enough to Gunn to touch him. He felt her leg brush against his, a soft breast push against his arm. She was trembling.

"It's all over," he said quietly.

"I—we can't stay in there anymore," said Janice. "I'd be too terrified."

"Let's build the fire up and pack up," said Gunn. "Meredith, can you bring up the horses? I'll saddle the one up."

The horses were still stamping and whinnying, the smell of cougar strong in their nostrils.

"I'll take care of 'em," said Yancy, starting off.

Gunn walked with the women to the dying fire.

Janice held onto him. Amity stayed close.

"Thank you," whispered Janice. "I thought we were going to be eaten alive by that animal."

In the faint light from the coals, her eyes were misty, her lips wet. He turned away from her, shocked at the look of raw desire in her eyes.

The sun came up hot, blistering, boiling the air, sending heat waves shimmering over the land like scalding steam. The road led through deep gullys and washed-out creek beds. At times, the old stage trail rose up and continued over ancient walls made by people nobody remembered. The land was thick with mesquite timber, a scraggly beard of stunted, twisted wood that seemed to go on interminably.

Gunn led the way, keeping the horses going at a brisk pace, despite the heat. For some time now he had been aware that they had company—a lone Apache, dogging their trail like a shadow. He didn't say anything to the others. No need to alarm them. As far as he knew, there was only one and he kept the same distance. He had seen him only once or twice, out of the corner of his eye. Another time, on a rugged hill, the Apache's pony had skidded, throwing up a thin scrim of dust. So, the brave was there, following them, watching them, keeping track of them.

Flash floods had washed out the road in places, but the heat was already drying up the moisture, sucking it out of the ground and out of their bodies. The women were hungry, tired, sweating in the heat that was like a blacksmith's fire.

They came into the valley of the San Pedro, a vast open space cut through by a small remnant of what once must have been a mighty river. The contrast with the bluffs that bordered the abrupt end of the plain was startling. Beyond the towering bluffs, Gunn planned to make his move. This was the heart of Apache country. No man lived here. No white man. Even though some said the valley was fertile, it was desolate and remote. It was ringed by hiding places, and a man settling here might never get out alive. It was a domain for lizards and scorpions, and the San Pedro River was no more than a trickle in the summer sun.

They crossed the Cienega, which appeared to have been swallowed up by some underground maw. Now, where they crossed, its white sandy bed was dry as bone, blinding in the dazzle of the sun. Tall salt grass sprouted everywhere on the plain and dying sunflowers stood with bent heads, bright spots of yellow in a flowerless land, their big brown eyes glazed over with dust. Huge cactus plants lent an air of unreality to the landscape, their thick bodies bristling with spines. And beyond were the mountains, the path to them hard on the horses. The animals would have to climb and wade through heavy sand. A perfect place for Gunn to drop off and wait for the lone Apache who had now dropped miles behind them and moved slowly, using the little cover available.

Gunn pulled up in a thicket of cactus that rose a dozen feet in the air. The trunks were two feet thick.

"You'll have to go on to Tucson without me," he said abruptly.

"What?" Janice looked at him as he climbed down. She sat there with a helpless expression on her face.

"Look," he said, "I think you'll be all right. But we've got company. An Apache has been following us since we left Dragoon Springs. He was probably close by all night."

Amity's face blanched.

Yancy frowned.

"What are you going to do?"

"Try and find out why he's following us. Maybe see what Sangre is up to. We haven't seen any smoke and no war parties. It's just awful damned quiet all of a sudden."

"But—but—" sputtered Janice.

Gunn reached into his pocket and took out some bills.

"I know you don't have any money. Here's some until you can send a wagon back for your things. Don't worry about it. And, I'd like to give you that document. Show it to the law in Tucson first and then to any army that might be there. Can I trust you, Miss Longworth?"

"As much as I can trust you," she snapped.

A shadow flitted inside Gunn's pale eyes.

"I'm sorry," she said. "I—I didn't mean that."

Gunn handed her the document.

"If I get through," he said, "I'll go to the Sunset Hotel. It's a run-down flea bag, but I can trust them there. If you need to get in touch with me, I'll be there."

Gunn walked over to Yancy and looked up at him. He pulled out some more bills.

"Meredith, if you'd take my horse to a livery and get him shod, I'd be most grateful. If I don't show up in a week, he's yours."

"Why, thank you, Gunn. But how will you get back? You can't walk it."

"I can walk it. Now get going. I don't want that Apache to know I'm dropping off here. Just follow the road. Stay out of those Spanish bayonets. They'll ruin a horse's legs. Don't leave the road, and don't stop."

Amity looked down at him, softened by his leaving.

"Good-bye," she said. "I hope you make it."

Janice turned away so that he could not see the emotion on her face. She was trying hard not to cry.

"No matter what happens," she husked, "I'll always be grateful to you for saving our lives last night."

150

"Go on."

Gunn watched them ride away. Janice looked back, but Gunn was no longer there. He had brushed out his tracks and was climbing behind a towering heap of rocks. There, he would wait for the Apache, hoping to hell the wind didn't blow his scent into the brave's snout. For the next hour or so, he would be a lizard, basking in the sun. He would be invisible, listening. He would wait for as long as he had to wait. He would be an Apache.

He had no water and no food; he had only the clothes on his back, his pistol, and his rifle.

But he had something else, too.

He knew where the Apache was. He knew that the Apache would come.

Capt. Jonathan Rice had learned to live in the desert with his handicap. He was blond, blue eyed, and the sun was a deadly poison to him. Or had been. Rice, however, was resourceful and quick. He learned. He studied. He asked questions. He experimented. He had experimented with various plant dyes to protect his skin, and they said that in the field he wore paint just like any Injun. In a sense, this was true. He was always trying out a new vegetable dye, smearing it on his face when out in the field.

The men had taken to calling him "War Paint," and the Pima and Apache, knowing what he looked like, called him "El Rubio Pinto." The painted blond.

Rice didn't mind these appellations.

He was a man totally dedicated to doing his job. He followed orders. No, he went beyond that. He made a creative effort out of following orders. He was spit and polish all the way, but he was a thinking man's soldier. When he was given a job to do, he found ways to do that job better than anyone else.

That's what he was trying to do now.

Months ago he had heard friendly Pimas tell him about Sangre and certain white men who were friends of the Apache. At first, he had thought this was just talk, but the Pimas sent out scouts and took an Apache brave prisoner. So, Rice had talked to a man he had met two years before who could help. This was Choya. Now he had learned from a Pima Indian that Choya had been killed. He had also learned that Sangre's band had repeating rifles. And the name Jennings kept coming up. And Kelly.

Jacob Hallman stepped down a stair to greet Rice.

"Hello Jon. I didn't know you were in Tucson. Thought you were over to the Gila."

"I was. Can we talk Jake?"

"Sure. Now?"

"Yes. The saloon'll be fine."

Rice gave orders to the men with him, and dismounted. He and Hallman went inside the Tecolote, and found a table at the back. It was hot and the place stank of sweat, beer, mezcal, tequila, and cheap wine.

Rice ordered beer from the *mozo*. Hallman wanted whiskey, but told the waiter to bring him *pulque*.

"You're hurt," said Rice, as Hallman sipped from the bottle of laudanum. "We have a surgeon in town."

"Thanks, Jon. I'll see him later. You heard the news?"

"I heard. Apaches jumped you. Sangre. You had rifles."

"For the Pima scouts. As you ordered."

"I ordered Henrys. Winchesters."

"I got a better deal on the Spencers."

"Or Sangre did."

Rice's blue eyes were noncommittal. His brushy blond moustache twitched with a slight tic. He was a short man, but he gave the impression of size. His shoulders were wide, his arms beefy. His body held not an ounce of spare fat. He was tough from being in the field, from hard soldiering.

"Jon, are you trying to tell me something?"

The *mozo* brought the beer. The two men looked at each other. Rice's eyes were steady on Hallman's.

"I don't know yet, Jake. I had a man in with Jennings. A breed. He's dead and there's smoke all along the Butterfield Trail."

Hallman winced as he moved his wounded arm.

"We gave Sangre full measure."

"Tell me what happened, Jake."

Hallman told him about the attack, about Gunn.

"You think this Gunn is in cahoots with Sangre?"

"I don't know, Jon. He drove me off at gunpoint. He's got a price on his head. He's a killer."

"Choya was about to get the goods on Jennings. He was killed before we could find out much."

"I think it's Gunn you're after. Mighty funny him being on that stage."

"You've got a point, Jake."

The men drank. Rice got up suddenly and put a coin on the table.

"You leaving, Jon?"

"I'm going to send out a patrol, get some scouts over toward the San Pedro, and see what young St. John has to say about the attack."

"Mind you keep an eye out for Gunn."

"I will."

Hallman watched the captain go. His head swung around and his eyes met Jennings's at the bar. Hallman nodded. Jennings and Kelly came over and sat at the table.

"How'd it work out?" asked Jennings.

"Your name came up, but you got to Choya in time."

"Damn. I don't like all these soldiers in Tucson," said Jennings.

"Me neither," said Kelly. Both men had whiskies. "It don't look good for Sangre."

"You leave that to me," said Hallman. "Before nightfall, Rice will have plenty to do. There's another ranch this side of St. John's. Even as we talk, Sangre ought to be hitting it. They'll let a couple get away to spread the word."

"You're plenty slick," said Kelly.

They were interrupted by a woman's shout, and a commotion at the door. A knot of men parted and a Mexican woman charged straight for their table.

"Asesinos Cabrones!" she shouted, in Spanish. "You bastards! You killed my brother."

"Shit," said Jennings. "That's Ben Aquilar's sister."

"Get out of here," said Hallman quickly. "I'll take care of her."

Jennings and Kelly got up and slipped through the back door. A *mozo* tried to stop the woman, but she brushed him aside.

"Where is he?" she demanded. "Where's Jennings?"

Hallman stood up.

"There's no one here by that name," he told the woman.

Clarita Aquilar stood there, her dark eyes flashing, smoking with rage. She was small, no more than twenty-two or twenty-three, with long, raven-sleek hair, even white teeth, and an oval face that was light bronze. She wore a red ribbon in her hair, and a long, multicolored dress tied at the waist.

"He is here. He killed my brother."

"Strong words, ma'am," said Hallman.

She drew a knife. The men around her stepped backward to form a wide circle.

"Are you a friend of his?" she asked.

154

"I know him."

"You tell him, if I see him, I kill him. First, I cut off his *cojones.*"

"Better put that knife away," said Hallman. "You're scaring all these grown men."

The laughter broke the tension.

Clarita looked around her at the men and flushed with embarrassment. She sheathed the knife under her belt, whirled, and raced back outside.

"Now there's a Mexican spitfire," said a man at the bar.

"I'd hate to be Jennings if she catches up with him," said another.

"Damn right. She scared hell out of you, Tom. Ain't nothin' worse'n a she-cat with a blade."

The laughter diminished. Glasses clinked.

Hallman stood there, a scowl beginning to darken his face. He felt as if he had a strong rope in his hands. It had been working fine. Now, he could feel it slowly start to unravel.

CHAPTER FOURTEEN

Gunn felt the sweat soak into the back of his shirt and trickle down his sides. The sweatband of his hat filled up, overflowed, dripped stinging moisture into his eyes. Yet he didn't move. The rock beneath him turned warm and the glare from the stone burned his eyes to slits. His legs ran with sweat and his palms turned oily.

Yet he knew the Apache would spot the slightest movement.

The minutes dragged by, stretching until they seemed like hours. He listened for any alien sound.

The sun crawling across the sky seemed to focus down on him, magnifying the heat, turning the rocks into an oven.

The heat struck the rocks and bounced back into his face, smothering him. His mouth dried up, his throat filled with sand. He knew he could not last much longer. The Apache was taking his time, being careful. Gunn knew that he could not be seen from the road, but if the Indian circled or became suspicious, he was exposed. His boot rested near a bush growing out of the rocks. Another bush grew near his other knee. Even a slight movement of either bush could be seen from some distance in the clear air.

Finally, he heard the sound he had been waiting for: the faint tread of a horse's unshod hooves on stony ground. A rock rattled, then there was silence. The Apache was studying the tracks. Or looking ahead, up the slope. Gunn could almost feel the brave's eyes on him, boring into his back. He quelled the temptation to turn over and look behind him. He knew there was no one there. But the feeling of being watched persisted.

The hoofbeats sounded closer. Gunn resisted the urge to get up and throw down on the approaching warrior. Instead, his eyes sought out the Apache. Without moving his head, he peered over the rim of the rock. He saw a feather, then dark hair shining in the sun.

Then, he glimpsed the tops of bare shoulders.

The Apache moved a few feet closer.

Gunn braced himself, holding his breath.

The Apache stopped, and appeared to look straight at him. Gunn didn't bat an eyelash.

The Indian spoke to his pony, and began studying the ground. He moved closer. Gunn could smell him now, see the paint on his face, the marks on his arms. He let out a breath slowly and took another one.

The brave's pony moved a few feet closer.

Gunn lost sight of him, counted to five.

Then, he leaped up, raced to the edge of the rock, and leaped into the air. He let out a lusty yell, and swung his rifle in a half arc.

The Apache looked up, startled, and tried to bring up the Spencer rifle he carried across his lap.

Gunn's leap was perfect. He hit the Apache's side, ramming the butt of his Winchester into the Indian's chest. The pony spooked. The brave tumbled backward, Gunn atop him. The two men landed hard.

"Oooff!" grunted the Apache in an expulsion of air.

Gunn's momentum rolled him off the fallen warrior. His shoulder struck a rock. Pain surged through the ligaments and rattled the shoulder bone.

The Spencer clattered on the ground.

The Apache reached for it, struggling to suck air back into his lungs. Gunn lashed out with a boot, and kicked the butt. The rifle spun out of the Apache's grasp. The brave then reached for his boot knife. Gunn got up on one leg, and swung the rifle butt. He cracked the Indian in the shins.

The brave howled with pain.

Gunn stood up all the way and levered a shell into the chamber. He pointed the barrel at the Apache's head.

"Voy a matarte, si te mueve," he growled. "If you move, I'll kill you."

The Apache froze. No fear showed in his face. Instead, his eyes glittered with a fierce hatred.

In Spanish, Gunn asked questions.

"Your name?"

"Chamaco."

"Why are you following me?"

"Sangre wants to know where you are. He wants to kill you himself."

"Where is Sangre?"

No answer.

Gunn brought back a boot, then buried the toe in the Apache's crotch. The dark eyes fogged over, but the Indian made no sound.

"Again, Chamaco. Where is Sangre?"

The young brave looked up, moved his head. Gunn saw it. Black smoke rising over the horizon. Another ranch.

"Where does your chief go now?"

Chamaco shook his head.

"I'll mash your balls to powder if you don't tell me. Where are you meeting Sangre?"

"Near the white man's town. Tucson."

"When?"

"Tomorrow."

Gunn stepped back and eased the hammer down. He had let one Apache go and things might have been different now if he hadn't. Sangre was alive, seeking revenge. But this Apache was well named. Chamaco. He was just a boy, probably not a good warrior yet. Gunn would not kill him.

"You tell Sangre I will meet him on the Gila in five days. I will be at the rancho of Don Diego Villegas. I will kill him then."

"You filth. Sangre will hang your scalp from his belt."

Gunn swung the rifle just hard enough. The butt struck Chamaco in the head. He folded up, unconscious. Satisfied, Gunn walked over and picked up the Spencer. He broke the stock on a boulder, then hammered the barrel into useless metal. He threw the rifle into the brush. He whistled for the Apache pony. It stood, rope bridle trailing in the dust, a hundred yards away. Gunn stalked up to him slowly, speaking in Spanish. The pony stayed until he got right up to it then tossed its head and stamped its foot.

"Calmate, caballo!" he soothed. *"Esperame un momentito."*

The pony stayed as Gunn slowly grasped its bridle. He mounted, his legs dangling underneath the bareback pinto. He headed the pony up the trail. Behind him, Camacho stirred. Gunn was not worried. An Apache could walk all day and all night. He would find Sangre and give him the message. If Sangre had any honor, he would be at the Villegas ranch in five days.

The problem was, would he be able to make it? With Esquire under him, he might. And he must get there before Sangre. Diego Villegas was the man behind

159

Jacob Hallman. It was his letter that outlined the scheme to drive out all the ranchers and buy up their lands cheap. It was a bold move, but Villegas wouldn't expect him. He knew the place. It was vast and open. There, Sangre and his braves would have no place to hide. It was not Apache country, but Pima territory. The Pima and the Apache were deadly enemies.

She was waiting for him at the Sunset Hotel.

She wore a veil over her face, and sat in a dark corner of the shabby lobby, so that at first he did not recognize her. Gunn walked up to the desk, put money on the counter, and signed the register as William Gunnison, El Paso. The clerk, a Mexican, didn't even look at his name.

"One night," said Gunn.

"Two dollars."

"High."

"The best room. It has a window. It is easy to get out of."

Gunn took his change. The woman came over to him.

"Gunn. I've been waiting for you."

"Janice?"

"Please, not now. I—I may have been followed."

The clerk rattled a key on the counter. Gunn picked it up, read the wooden board. The room was downstairs, at the back. D.

"Come on," he said, grabbing Janice's arm.

He had ridden the pinto hard, watered briefly, stolen into Tucson after dark. He turned the pony loose, and went straight to the hotel. All day long he had avoided Pima scouts and army patrols. Once, he had seen three Apaches riding northwest. Close to Tucson, he had heard horses coming fast and had hidden until they passed. News of the ranch burning, no doubt. The horses had been shod, but it was no patrol. Survivors, perhaps.

Tucson was a small town of humble adobes, few Americans, lots of Mexicans. Gunn knew that the name was derived from a Pima phrase, *Sluyk-son,* which meant dark brown spring. Pima, Papago, and Sobaipuri peoples had lived there before the coming of the Spanish. Tonight it was a restless town, full of soldiers and Pima scouts. The Sunset was a small place, just out of the center of town. Safe enough for a short while. Gunn opened the door to the room, leaned his rifle against the wall, and struck a match. Janice followed him in, closing the door. He found a lamp and lit it.

"I'm surprised you're here," he said.

"You won't be when I tell you what's happened."

Gunn tossed his hat on the bed, sat down in a chair, and took off his boots.

Janice sat in a chair and removed her veil.

"You need a bath," she commented.

"And a shave. Some grub."

"I have your saddlebags in my room at the Tucson Hotel. Your saddle's at the livery. Your horse is shod. Meredith took care of that. But I wouldn't try and pick him up, if I were you. A man named Kelly is watching the livery."

"Oh, you know about Kelly."

Janice Longworth let out a sigh. She smelled nice, Gunn thought. He knew how he smelled. He was caked with sweat and dust. The bed felt good. He wanted to lie in it and sleep for a week.

"I know about a lot of things—now," she said quietly.

161

"Hallman here?"

"Yes. He was here. I think he's gone. The soldiers are looking for him. He is a snake, isn't he? He lied about you. He said you killed Ned Wales. Shot him in the back."

"I didn't."

"None of us thinks so. But we can't prove it."

"What did you do with the paper I gave you?"

"I showed it to the newspaper and they made a copy of it. Then I took it to Captain Rice. He asked me where I got it and I told him. When I mentioned your name, he didn't believe me. That is, he thinks you may have forged it."

"Didn't he take Yancy's word?"

"No. Yancy looks up to you. That's obvious. Rice said he had a case of hero-worship."

Gunn cursed under his breath.

It was important for Rice to be at the Villegas Ranch when Sangre came. For Hallman, too. He had no doubt that he'd find Hallman there. The only thing he had in his favor was the element of surprise.

"I'm sorry, Gunn. I think you're being misunderstood."

"I'll need those saddlebags, and some grub. I'll have to ride out tomorrow."

"Where are you going?"

"You can tell Rice I'm meeting Sangre at Don Diego Villegas's ranch. He'll understand that."

"But aren't you—won't you be in trouble if the captain finds you there?"

"Ma'am, I'm in trouble now."

Clarita Aguilar waited in the shadows across the street from the Sunset Hotel. She saw the white woman leave the hotel and walk toward the street that lead to the Tucson where she was staying. She had been following her all evening, saw the tall stranger check in, and the two walk back to his room. She had heard talk of Gunn all day and was convinced that this was the man. Perhaps he was the man to help her.

She walked briskly into the hotel, asked the clerk in Spanish for the room of the man known as Gunn.

"No Gunn here. Gunnison. He's in D."

Clarita knocked on his door a few seconds later.

"Back already?" said Gunn, opening the door.

"Please, don't say anything until I finish talking," said Clarita, brushing past him.

Gunn shut the door behind her.

"Do you know a man named Jennings?"

"I know who he is."

"He is going to kill Captain Rice tonight, after a late supper at the Tucson Hotel."

Gunn let out a breath.

"Who are you?"

"Jennings murdered my brother. In El Paso. I want revenge."

"Where is Jennings?"

"He is hiding in the back of the Tecolote Saloon. In one hour, he is going to the Tucson Hotel and shoot Captain Rice dead."

"How do you know all this?"

"I have friends. Even now, there is another man hunting you. His name is Kelly. He is at the livery."

Gunn believed her.

"Take me to Jennings," he said.

"You will kill him?"

"I will stop him, if I can. When I find him, you must tell Captain Rice about this. Savvy?"

"I understand."

"Come. I will leave a note for the woman who is bringing me food and my saddlebags."

"I am most grateful to you."

"I haven't done anything yet."

"But you will. I have heard much about you. Much that is good, much that is bad."

"And you think I will help you?"

"The good things tell me you will."

Gunn borrowed a pencil and paper at the desk, left a note for Janice Longworth. The note merely said he'd be back soon.

Clarita left Gunn at the back door of the Tecolote.

He watched her go, then checked his pistol. It was loaded, all six chambers. He gave her ten minutes, then went in the back door of the saloon. There was a small storeroom, and another room off the hall. He heard voices. He recognized one of them. Jennings.

Light leaked from under a door. The voices came from behind the door.

He waited, listening. Two men were talking. Maybe more were there, but they did not talk.

Gunn put his ear to the door.

"Abe, you really gonna bust that captain?"

"Sure am, Pedro. You ride on to Don Diego's when I'm done and tell Hallman it's finished."

"Where you go after that?"

"I'm meetin' Sangre."

"He is near?"

"He is. You pack that tequila good, hear? I got a long ride."

"What about Kelly?"

"Tell him to get Gunn before he leaves." There was the scraping sound of a chair. "I got to get over to the

164

hotel now. I won't be back. Anybody asks, you ain't seen me."

Gunn heard the sound of coins clinking on the table, the rustle of paper money. He stepped back in the shadows.

The door opened.

A man's frame filled the doorway. Light spilled over his shoulders.

"Jennings?" Gunn whispered.

"Who's there?"

"Gunn."

Jennings dropped his saddlebags, and knifed his hand toward his holster in a quick movement.

Leather creaked as Gunn's hand smoothly drew his Colt free of its sheath. The loud click boomed in the hall.

"Jesus!" exclaimed Jennings, his pistol halfway out of its holster. "I ain't gonna make it."

The sound of an exploding cartridge drowned out Jennings's words. He clutched his belly as blood spread out from a dark hole. He leaned against the doorjamb, sagging.

Gunn fired again.

Jennings took the second slug in the heart.

He was dead before his body thudded to the floor.

There was dead silence in the saloon.

"Well, Pedro, you want any of that?" asked Gunn.

A voice came from inside the room, a voice quavering with fear.

"No, *señor,* I do not even know this man. I do not know you. I have not seen you nor heard of you. Whoever you are."

Gunn suppressed a laugh.

He eased the hammer down on the Colt and holstered it.

Then, he stalked out the back door and walked toward the Sunset.

Janice was there, in his room, waiting.

She did not know that he had just killed a man. His saddlebags were on the table. There was food. Her valise was at the foot of the bed. She sat on the far edge of the bed, in shadow, her back to him. She had been looking out the window. Now, the shade was pulled, and the lamp was burning low. He could see only the bare outline of her body.

"I saw Amity and Meredith. They know you are here. They both agreed to tell no one. I think Amity's changed her mind about you."

"And you?"

She pointed to her valise.

"I'll spend the night."

"No. Someone might come looking for me."

"Who?"

"Kelly. Or Rice."

"Here?"

"A lot of people know where I am now. One of them might let it slip."

"Not Meredith or Amity."

"No. Maybe not them."

"Who else, then, Gunn?"

"I don't know."

Jennings was dead, but Clarita had gone to Rice. She might tell him. He might force it out of her. There was no way to prove that Jennings was going to try and shoot Rice. Only Clarita knew, and it was the word of a Mexican carrying a grudge.

"I'm staying," said Janice.

She rose from the bed and walked toward him. She slipped a thin robe off her shoulders.

Gunn stared.

Janice Longworth was naked underneath the robe.

He stood there and his jaw dropped as the robe whispered to the floor.

"I want you," she said. "Most desperately."

Gunn swallowed hard.

In the lamp glow, she was beautiful.

CHAPTER FIFTEEN

Gunn forgot his hunger for food.

Janice slinked toward him, her firm uptilted breasts bobbing as she walked. Her flesh was flawless, pure. The dark golden thatch between her legs was in stark contrast to the alabaster whiteness of her skin.

She put her arms around his neck, and drew his lips to hers.

He felt her push her loins into his as her lips crushed against his mouth. Her tongue parted his lips, darting inside. Heat suffused his loins. Her scent clogged his nostrils. She smelled like woman and like little desert flowers. Her kiss was warm and wet. Her body clung to his, pressing him with its surging heat.

"You push a man hard," he said, breaking the kiss.

She breathed on his face, and tightened her arm's grip around his neck.

"Too hard, Janice. Let up."

Her leg twined around his.

Gunn looked into her eyes.

Her blue eyes were like tiny seas, fathomless, swarming with foam, frothing at the crests of wavelets—blue eyes that drew him into her depths. Her arm around his neck was soft, yet insistent. It was good to be touched by a woman. It was good to feel a woman's touch, a touch that made the hairs on his arms crackle with static, made his loins melt, made his belly warm. It was good to feel her soft blond hair against his chin and smell the fragrance of the thick shocks that billowed up to his face. He wanted to sink into her hair, clasp her to him and drink of her.

"You got me off guard," he husked.

"Oh?"

"I have clothes on. You don't."

She sighed longingly, stroking his neck with loving fingers. A hand of hers razed his arm, savaged his stomach, tugged at his belt in a gesture of demand.

"Urgh!" she crooned. "I love your body."

"Janice. Where did you come from?"

She stepped away from him and he grew giddy looking at her, wanting her. His pants bulged with his desire. She looked at him, looked at his discomfort, drew in a breath, and held it.

"Do you want me?" she asked simply.

Gunn threw back his head and cracked loose the tension in his neck. He snapped back to look at her again. A woman aglow in the faint gold light of the oil lamp, a woman stark naked and willing, with a body like a fine painting. A body to be tasted like good wine. The golden thatch between her legs now looked like spun silk, pale blond in the sidelight that threaded through it. This was a woman standing here and she shimmered like someone he had dreamed of on hard lonesome trails. She reflected light and dreams until something inside him ached for her, until a hardness in him softened and wanted her so much he might kill to possess her.

"Go to the bed," he gruffed, his voice uncertain, trembling. "I'll be there in a minute."

Janice's eyes opened. She smiled without showing

her teeth. She drifted backward to the bed, her gaze never leaving Gunn's face.

Gunn sat down, worked his boots off, then peeled out of his clothes. He strode to the bed, as naked as she, and climbed in beside her. She opened her arms and they embraced. He kissed her face, then moved to her lips. Her body melded to his, squirming as it sought contact. His bone-hard cock, flattened against her diaphragm, seeped precoital juices. Her hand slid down his side, found his cock, squeezed around it. Blood rushed to the veins, engorging them even more.

"Oh, Gunn," she breathed. "I've been thinking about this every night. I couldn't get you out of my mind."

He stroked her breasts, toying with the nipples. Her hair, brushed back from her face, shimmered in the coppery light. Her blue eyes sparkled with a dazzling magnetism. Her soft breasts were firm, the nipples pink, swollen. He traced the dark aureoles, and felt her body quiver against his. Her hand tightened on his cock and began to move up and down.

"You make me want you bad," he husked.

"I already want you so much I'm like jelly inside."

He kissed her breasts, tonguing the nipples.

"Oh," she cried, as a tremor rippled through her.

He rolled away, and moved his head to the nest between her legs.

"Oh, please do that to me," she begged.

He spread her legs wide, and smoothed aside the wiry blond hairs of her thatch. He kissed her puffy lips and tongue stroked the slit until she undulated with pleasure. His tongue slipped between the labials, stroking the satiny inner lining. Her hands locked onto his head, fingers threaded in his hair. He nudged her pubic bone with his nose, and pried her sex until the lips widened. His mouth found the tiny clitoral protuberance. He tongued it, then suckled it. She bucked as if a charge of electricity had surged through her. She screamed softly, from far away.

He worried the clit-trigger until she cried out with the pain.

"I—it got so tender," she explained breathlessly. "But, oh, you don't know what you did to me." She stroked his hair. He moved up her body, sliding over it until they were face to face, their loins fitted together. His cock waited at the portal, seeping warm fluid through its eyelet. "I never imagined anything could be this good."

"Do you still want me?"

"Yes, oh yes, more than ever. I want to feel you inside me. Every inch of you."

He slid inside, his bony muscle parting her flesh, sinking into the steaming heat of her sex. She gasped, and buckled with pleasure. Her hands flailed the air, then rested on his back. She massaged him as he burrowed deeper. She was not a virgin. He slid still deeper.

Janice's eyes opened and looked into his.

"I got away from Miss Bangs once, back in finishing school," she said. "The girls there talked about this all the time. Until I wanted it so much I had to find out what it was like."

"You don't have to explain."

"It wasn't like this. It wasn't anything like this. He was a mere boy. As inexperienced as I was. It lasted only a minute."

"That's not long enough," he said.

"No, Gunn. With you, nothing is long enough."

She bucked with a sudden orgasm as he slid back up her tunnel. And again, as he slid back down. Her eyes filmed over, then closed. Her flesh shook, the muscles in her legs quivering as a deep shuddering spasm gripped her. Again and again she climaxed, until her

171

honeypot was drenched with flooding juices.

Gunn could no longer stay himself. He gripped her with strong hands, and began to plunge in and out of her soaked pussy, plumbing her depths with savage speed.

Slap, slap, slap.

Janice moaned, matching his urgent rhythm.

Gunn lost himself in the primitive compulsion that drove him now. It was as if his swollen shaft was smacking into her on its own. Janice's legs bounced like rubbery appendages out of control. Her eyes rolled in their sockets. She began to croon as her orgasms linked up in a convulsive series of spasms until they were chained together in a single, thought-shattering climax.

"Oh, oh, oh—" she shrieked, mindlessly.

"Now!" Gunn exclaimed, the seed in his pouch disgorging in a milky flood. He held onto her arms as a massive shudder shook his body like a towel flapping on a line. Surf roared in his ears, blood pounded in his temples. A flood of weakness washed through him, draining his strength, turning him limp even as his cock spewed its last gouts of seed.

He fell on her, spent, like a man washed up by the tide.

Janice held him tightly, rocking him in her grateful embrace.

And the night was theirs alone, for then, for an eternity.

Maj. Jamison Heller, his dark hair slicked down and parted in the middle, sat stiff in the chair. The hotel restaurant was deserted except for the military men seated at a large round table in the center of the room. Fluted glass lamps flickered on the walls, and a large one with a painted glass shade spilled light on their empty plates.

Capt. Jonathan Rice wiped his mouth and turned to his aide.

"Lieutenant Nevins, get over there to the Tecolote and see if this woman's story bears up."

Heller pushed away from the table, snapping his fingers for a cigar. His aide, Lieutenant Stonecipher, opened a box, and offered it to his superior. Heller took one and bit off the end. Stonecipher passed the box over to Rice, who shook his head.

"Please, Captain. It may be the last cigar we share together. More brandy, Stonecipher."

Brandy was poured.

"Do you believe her?" asked Rice, taking a cigar.

"The letter looks authentic. Now, with this information, it just may be that we can move on the Villegas *rancheria* and catch the Apache off his home ground."

"I speak the truth," said Clarita. "This Gunn is *mucho hombre.*"

"The Pima scouts, sir," ventured Donald Stonecipher.

"Yes, the scouts say that Sangre and his band scattered after that last burning, heading west," said Heller. He was a stocky man, with pouches under his eyes, and a military bearing that was out of place on the frontier. His soft hands bespoke a desk job at the Presidio in San Francisco.

"It could be that this Gunn is not what he's appeared to be," said Rice. "And we can't locate Jacob Hallman."

"I'd feel a lot better about my daughter being here in Tucson if we marched on the Villegas *rancheria,"* said Heller, sipping his brandy.

"Amity is a most charming young lady," said Rice. "She, too, seems to think this Gunn is on the up and up.

173

But we do have a flyer on the man. He's been convicted of murder up in Wyoming."

"I know all that, Jon. Hell, if we locked up every murderer, we'd lose half of the cavalry."

Muted laughter rippled around the table.

"We'd have to leave troops in Tucson," said Rice, lighting Heller's cigar, and then his own, with a long taper.

"Of course. A dozen men. We'll field a dozen. Use the Pima scouts." Heller's brow wrinkled in thought. He wore a full brushy beard and his mouth moved inside it like an animal's mouth. His lips were wet with brandy. The waiters began clearing the table, clanking plates.

"How long would it take us to get to Villegas's?" asked Heller, when the waiters had left.

"Five days if we pushed it. Surely, you would stay here, sir. You must be tired after your journey from Mariposa Wells."

Heller waved his cigar in disagreement.

"Nonsense. I want to be in on the finish. You've done a good job, Jon, but this looks like the showdown we've been wanting. If Hallman gets away with his scheme it would take years for this country to return to normal. We can't let him stir up these Apaches any more. And Sangre is just too smart even for your Pimas."

"I agree," said Rice. "I thought we'd catch him off guard, but Hallman has mucked up our plans."

Clarita smiled.

"Then you will go after Hallman? He is as guilty of murdering my brother as Jennings."

"I think you may be assured, Miss Aguilar, that we will do our best, providing your story about Jennings bears up."

As if to punctuate his words, Lieutenant Nevins returned, out of breath.

"Make your report, lieutenant," said Rice.

"Yes, sir. A man named Jennings was shot in a back room of the Tecolote Cantina. A man named Gunn is said to have done the deed. No one saw him, but a witness heard him identify himself."

"Where is this Gunn now?" asked Heller.

"No one knows. No one wants to talk much about the killing, sir."

"Very good." Heller stood up, tossing his lap napkin in a heap. He swigged a final draught of brandy.

Rice and Stonecipher rose from their chairs.

"Jon, can we outfit and take the field by noon tomorrow?"

"We can, sir."

"Gentlemen, let's give the orders and go to our quarters. Miss Aguilar, I bid you good evening."

Clarita rushed away, too ecstatic to reply.

Heller chuckled.

"She's probably running right back to Gunn," he said.

"Want someone to follow her?" asked Rice.

"No, Jon. If this expedition doesn't work out, we'll have a long ride for nothing. Gunn is not important at this stage. Besides, our man was a damned hero at Missionary Ridge. Captain Gunnison. William Gunnison."

"I remember," said Rice. "Odd that a man like him would go bad."

"Not so odd. Jacob Hallman was a colonel in the cavalry and now he's a no-account renegade."

Jon Rice shook his head, then straightened his tunic.

The only good man in this whole bunch had been Eugenio Salazar—Choya. And he was dead. If for no other reason, Rice wanted justice for Choya.

*   *   *

175

Mick Kelly's snoring woke him up at dawn.

Or something else did.

He blinked, and sat up from the pile of straw. The livery stable was quiet; the stale air was thick with the acrid reek of urine and the musty scent of horse dung.

It was quiet, but there had been a noise.

A horse banging against a stall?

Pale light filtered through the high windows and the cracks in the huge doors.

Kelly picked up his rifle. The barrel was cold. He shivered. He shook straw off his sleeve and brushed the clinging stuff from his trousers. He had slept most of the night. He stepped out of the empty stall, and glanced at the Tennessee Walker. Gunn's horse. He breathed with relief.

"Kelly?"

The voice came from nowhere.

Kelly jerked around, raising the rifle.

"Who in hell is it? Abe, is that you?"

"Abe Jennings is dead."

"Who killed him? Who are you? Show your face, mister."

"I killed him, Kelly."

"You—you're not—"

Gunn stepped out of the shadows near the door that opened onto the street. His Winchester was leveled at Kelly's gut.

"I'm Gunn. Remember me?"

"Jesus, Gunn. You got the drop on me. I ain't even got this cocked."

Gunn set the Winchester against a stall partition.

Kelly moved. He crouched, and levered the Spencer carbine. For a moment, he thought he was going to make it.

Then, Gunn's hand flashed down to his pistol. He filled his hand in a split second. Kelly's jaw dropped, his mouth opening in surprise.

He heard the click of Gunn's hammer as his finger moved into the trigger guard. Everything seemed to slow down. He saw the pistol sprout smoke, and then flame made an orange hole in the smoke, and the Colt quivered as it bucked in Gunn's hand.

The ball caught him under the chin. In the neck.

Kelly spluttered, then tried to speak.

The word, whatever it was, just squeaked through blood, coming out as a bubbling croak.

The Spencer dropped from his hands without ever going off. He lifted up a hand, not to his throat, but to the ceiling. To the sky, to heaven.

Then he fell, his knees buckling, his legs swaying out from under him.

He hit the hard-packed ground with a thud.

Gunn stepped over to him, ejecting the spent shell into his palm. He reloaded, watching Kelly until the man stopped breathing. It was over in two minutes. Kelly twitched for three more minutes after Gunn dragged him into the straw-filled, empty stall.

He stepped outside, retrieved his packed saddlebags, and saddled Esquire quickly.

He filled a pouch with grain, corn, and wheat, and put it into his saddlebags. He sheathed the Winchester, and led Esquire outside.

Meredith Yancy was there, a pistol on his belt, a sack of food slung over his shoulder.

"Can I go with you, Gunn?"

"If you can catch up to me. I'm riding west."

Yancy's face lit up.

"I'm coming. Wait'll you hear what I know."

"There's a dead man in there, Meredith. And in five minutes, people are going to start asking a lot of questions. If you want to come along, you'd better saddle up quick."

Yancy needed no urging. He raced inside the livery as Gunn put his boot into the stirrup.

He rode out of Tucson before the crimson sun cleared the horizon.

Esquire's new shoes clicked reassuringly on the stones. The trail stretched for forty miles to Picacho Pass. Gunn touched spurs to Esquire and the horse steadied into a mile-eating gait.

The sun rose and Gunn felt the warmth on his back.

An hour later, Yancy rode beside him, grinning from ear to ear.

CHAPTER SIXTEEN

Chamaco watched Gunn ride away.

Moments later, the young white man rode off too, following the gray-eyed man. The brave grunted to the three others with him. He spoke softly in Apache.

"Make no sound. You, Pelon, come with me to get the women. Have the ponies ready for us, Amiguito."

Amiguito nodded. They had brought two extra ponies, and had stolen into the town the night before. After that, they had just watched. They knew where Amity and Janice were and Sangre's orders were clear. He wanted them as hostages when he found Gunn.

The braves led the ponies quietly past adobes that were still silent in the dawn. The unshod animals made no sound.

Chamaco and Pelon ran into the hotel. The lobby was empty. They knew the room where the women were staying. They leaped up the stairs soundlessly, and went to the door.

Chamaco knocked softly. Pelon stayed flattened against the wall, out of sight, but ready to move quickly.

The door opened a crack.

"Who—?" asked a sleep-drugged Amity.

Chamaco's arm shot out. His strong hand grabbed Amity's mouth, and clamped it shut. Pelon shoved past them and entered the room.

Janice was on the bed, half asleep.

Pelon grabbed her arms, jerked her up, and spun her around. He clamped a hand over her mouth. She screamed. Her scream was muffled. Pelon applied pressure and Janice sagged in his locking embrace.

Chamaco shoved Amity into the room.

She was wearing a flimsy, diaphanous nightgown. Janice wore cotton separates as pajamas—knickers and a blouse.

"You come," said Chamaco. "Put on dress. Ride."

Amity's eyes widened in horror as she looked at Janice. Janice steadied, but the light of fear danced in her eyes.

"You come now," said Chamaco. "No talk. We kill."

He loosened his grip on Amity's mouth.

"We'd better do what he says, Janice," she said.

Janice nodded, her blue eyes misting.

Pelon released her.

"No talk," he said, echoing Chamaco. "You die."

His tone was chilling. Janice nodded. She walked to the wardrobe, took out a riding outfit. She motioned for Amity to do the same. Both women were trembling with fear.

"I—" ventured Amity.

"Shush," whispered Janice. "Just get dressed. They want us alive. We have a chance."

"But how could they get in here and—?"

"No talk," repeated Chamaco, staying close to Amity. Pelon, too, was no more than a foot away.

The two Apaches watched the women dress. Their faces showed no expression, no emotion.

"Where are you taking us?" asked Janice.

"Where Gunn go," he said wisely.

"Then he is—"

"No, he isn't, Amity. I think we're being used as hostages. Don't fight them. Maybe we can help Gunn by cooperating."

"No talk," said Chamaco monotonously.

But they had no more trouble from the women. A few moments later, four Apaches and two white women were riding through hard country where stately saguaro stood like sentinels on the slopes, and barrel cactus rose like organ pipes in the morning mist. They would ride thirty miles farther than Gunn and Yancy, but they would do it quicker. They did not take the white man's road, but the old Apache trails that lead to the Gila, to the land of their enemies, the Pima.

Gunn and Yancy made Picacho Pass the first day, then stopped for water and sleep. A few brief rain squalls passed through during the night and the next day their horses drank water from ephemeral ponds that straddled the road. The mountains of the Sierra Madre dropped from view and they saw painted Pimas, faces black, lips blood red, riding toward the Gila without Apache scalps hanging from their lances. Forty miles beyond the pass, they encountered a band of more than a dozen Pimas butchering a beeve. The women wore beads, the men only breechcloths, faces painted for war. The two men rode on, then camped for the night, the Gila only a stretch of the legs away.

Yancy's heart quickened to see the Pimas at close hand. Gunn had to stop him from readying his Spencer every time they saw a brave in war paint.

"They look fierce," said Meredith.

"The Apache is their enemy. They live in the Maricopas in peace with the white man."

"What do they do besides fight Apaches?"

181

"They are farmers now. If the Apache would only look at the way the Pimas have learned to live, they might survive. But they are proud. They will fight to the last man and if they are not all killed, they will be driven out. Mexico won't have them and the New Mexicans are scared of them."

"Is it right to do this to the Apaches?"

"Men do this to other peoples. Instead of looking to the beauty of a place, they make war and drive out what they cannot understand. The Apache sees the land one way, the white man another. Since the Indian has not changed, has not accepted a conqueror, he must be destroyed."

"It's not fair."

"What is?" asked Gunn.

Clarita Aguilar caught up to Gunn and Yancy on the fourth day as the two men road toward the big bend of the Gila River. Her horse was lathered, near to foundering. They saw her first as a black dot on the horizon, a trace of dust in the sky. They waited, wondering who could be riding so fast in the heat.

Meredith cocked his rifle.

"No," said Gunn. "That's a woman. No Indian, either."

Clarita rode up, panting.

"Oh, *Dios mio,*" she exclaimed. "I have found you at last. Gunn, the soldiers are coming. You must wait for them."

"Hold on," said Gunn. "Get your breath. You ride that horse all the way from Tucson?"

"No, I have been on three horses. This is the man Yancy?"

Yancy nodded.

"The soldiers wondered if you had been captured too."

"Too?" asked Gunn.

"Two white women. Janice Longworth and the major's daughter, Amity Heller. The Apaches have them."

"No!" Yancy's face darkened.

"Yes. Major Heller is very angry. He brings many troops, has sent dispatches for more."

Clarita told them all she knew. The Apaches had been seen leaving Tucson with the white women. Major Heller had called up the troops and left at midmorning that same day. They had thought that Yancy had been killed or captured, as well.

"Why did you come here?" asked Gunn.

"Because they say you are going to Hallman. The blond woman, she was seen at the Sunset. The soldiers have asked a lot of questions. They think you put the Apaches up to capturing the women."

Gunn cursed.

"Go on back," he said to Clarita. "We're going on, to find Hallman."

"No! I will go with you. I can shoot and I have a rifle." She patted an old Henry hanging in a scabbard from her saddle.

"If your horse makes it, you can follow us," said Gunn. "But we'll not pack double."

"I will make it," she said defiantly, glaring at Gunn.

The Villegas rancho sprawled over a vast plain east of the Gila. From a rise, early in the morning on the fifth day, Gunn scanned the ranch house, the outbuildings, the fields, tawny and dry, spreading in every direction. Irrigation ditches threaded through the fields, but these were running with only a faint trickle. The Gila was down; the sand bars showed, and only sparse streams trickled past them. He lay flat on the hillock. His heart raced and something fluttered in his stomach when he saw the Apache camp by the river. He counted almost two dozen makeshift lodges, tents of cloth sewn from colored patches. Nothing moved. The heat seemed to have stripped the land of people. He saw ponies clustered around a mud hole. Cattle bawled, nosing the cracked earth in what were normally ponds. The hay grasses were burning up, dying from lack of water. The yellowing stalks rippled faintly in an arid breeze that fluttered across the fields.

Gunn crawled backward, careful not to stir up dust. Even though he could see no Apaches, they were there, inside their lodges, out of the baking heat. Insects buzzed like a pestilence, and the slight movement of air felt like a furnace door being opened. A lizard blinked at him from under a rock, its tongue lolling as it panted there in the shade.

Clarita and Yancy fanned themselves, using the horses for shelter from the merciless sun. Their faces were oiled with sweat, their clothes stained with it. Clarita wore a bandana over her head and her hair was dark with wetness. Yancy's face was burned raw from the glare and his hair was limp and straggly under his hat. Gunn looked the same, he knew. His hat was like a blotter that had been saturated. The sweatband had overflowed until the hat was like a rag dipped in water.

"Yes?" asked Clarita.

"We can do it," said Gunn. "It will take all our strength. It might kill us."

"What?" Yancy's voice was dry as a cornhusk.

"Burn them out. Forced them into the open. I want Hallman."

"What about Janice and Amity?"

184

"If Sangre has them, he'll use them," said Gunn.

"How?"

"He won't kill them, but he'll show them to me, so he can kill me."

Clarita shuddered. Gunn's eyes were like cold bullets.

Gunn plucked the petals from a dry cactus flower. He ground them to powder between his thumb and index finger. Then he held his hand high and dropped the dust, watching it carefully.

"The wind's blowing west, slightly northwest," he said. "Whatever you do, don't run that way once the shooting starts. Mark the sun's path, stay east of it. Now, both of you pay attention."

Gunn dropped to his knee, unsheathed his knife, and scraped a bare patch of earth about a foot in diameter. He made slashes, drew squares and circles. "Here's the Apache," he said, "here's the ranch house, here's the Gila. We will start our fires here and here, and we will meet at this point. Meredith, you and Clarita will see to it that they are cut off from the south. I don't want to have to set up a siege. I want to empty all those tepees and the house. And I want to face them on a narrow strip east of the Gila." Gunn explained how they would gather bundles of dry grass, tie them in shucks, and pull them behind the horses. They would each ride a long semicircle, and leave one narrow opening for those fleeing the fire to pass through.

"That's pretty brilliant," said Yancy.

"Let's get to it."

Gunn parted a manila rope until he had eight strands. He cut up one to tie the bundles. The others would be used to drag the flaming shucks through the high dry grass. When one burned out, another would

185

be ignited, dropped, and trailed. It was late afternoon when they finished. He sent Clarita and Meredith in a wide circle to their starting point, south of the ranch house and the Apache camp. He rode to a point north of the Apaches, out of sight.

He loaded his pockets with ammunition, counted long, estimating the time it would take the other two to get into position. Then, he lit the first bundle, and threw the still-burning match into a patch of dry grass. The breeze held. He dragged the bundle through the grasses. The fire caught. The air whipped at the flames. The flames spread, feeding on the air.

He rode fast, the bundle bouncing, throwing off sparks and scattering fire through the grasses. He saw smoke rise to the south, then to the east. He rode faster, cutting a wide circle. He lit two more bundles before he was finished. A wall of fire and smoke built up as the flames raced toward the Gila.

He met Meredith and Clarita, and dropped the last strand of rope. They ground tied their horses well away from the fire, but close enough to reach them should the breeze shift.

"Lie flat, shoot the Apaches when they come through," he said, positioning them so that they had good fields of fire.

Apaches appeared, riding their ponies through dark smoke. Gunn fired, knocking a brave down. Yancy's Spencer carbine barked. Clarita's battered Henry cracked. Men rushed from the house, and started beating at flames with blankets. The breeze picked up as the flames sucked up oxygen. The fire roared out of control, threatening to trap those in its path.

"Look!" cried Clarita, pointing.

Gunn saw the dust in the sky.

"Cavalry," he said.

Apaches came on foot and on pony. Gunn and the

others shot them, drove them in circles. The grasses hid them. Answering bullets whistled harmlessly overhead or thrashed through brush well in front of their positions. The opening narrowed. Choking Mexicans stumbled into view. They dropped their weapons when they heard the rifle fire and saw mounted Apaches tumbling from their ponies' backs.

"Wait!" called Gunn.

Jacob Hallman staggered through the opening. With him was a well-dressed Mexican, Sangre, Chamaco, and Pelon. Chamaco had Amity, Pelon had Janice.

Gunn stood up, so that he could be seen.

"Let us through," yelled Hallman, "or the girls die right here and now."

Gunn walked over to Yancy and dropped down. An Apache rode through. Clarita led him perfectly, fired, and the brave flew off the pony's back, skidding over scorched earth.

"Gunn! We'll cut their throats!"

Hallman and the others advanced slowly, coming into rifle range. Gunn let them come while he spoke to Yancy.

"Meredith," he said, "the cavalry will be here any minute. Once they come, Hallman will kill Janice and Amity, then try and shoot his way out. We have to kill those braves holding the women or they haven't got a chance. Can you take the one on the left? It has to be a clean head shot. I'll take the one on the right. One mistake and those girls get their throats slit."

"I don't know," he said. "I'm scared."

"They'll die if you aren't sure. After the Apaches have had their fun with them, they'll kill them. Settle down, now. Hallman is getting mighty impatient."

"What about Hallman?"

"I'll take care of him. Now, can you do it? You'll only get one chance. It has to be a perfect shot."

"All right. I'll do it."

"Gunn? You'd better give me an answer." Hallman held a pistol. Sangre carried a rifle. The Mexican, whom Gunn took to be Villegas, carried two pistols. The Apache braves held knives at the throats of the women, but carried rifles.

"We're going to surrender!" called Gunn.

Hallman said something and the party started forward. Behind them, Apaches ducked under smoke, waiting.

"Lift up your hands, but be ready to grab that Spencer," Gunn said to Yancy. "Is it cocked?"

"Cocked."

Hallman saw the hands raised, grinned. He favored his shoulder, but came on.

"Now!" said Gunn, under his breath. His hands dove for the Winchester. Yancy snatched up the Spencer. Gunn had already made his aim in his mind. Now, he brought the .44 to his shoulder, leveled it at Pelon, and fired. Pelon dropped. There was a bullet hole square in the middle of his forehead. Yancy shot Chamaco in the throat. The girls screamed and fell, pulled down by the weight of the stricken warriors.

Hallman cocked his pistol, and started to shoot Amity.

Gunn shot him. Pounding hoofbeats signaled the arrival of the cavalry. Sangre started to run toward Yancy. Gunn fired, but missed. Yancy fired. Clarita rose up and fired. Sangre tumbled head over heels. The cavalry charged from the north as the Apaches scattered, fleeing through the opening.

Hallman, wounded, staggered toward the girls.

"Stay down!" yelled Gunn, as he rose to his feet.

Hallman grabbed Amity, and started to limp off with her. Smoke and dust filled the air. Gunn caught up to Hallman, and jerked him away from Amity. Janice

188

got up, and started to run toward them. Hallman aimed his pistol at Gunn. Gunn shot him through the mouth, blowing out an eye and part of his brain.

Gunn grabbed the two women, guiding them through the smoke. The fat Mexican in the good clothes turned, and brought up both his pistols. Clarita shot him in the back. He stared at Gunn, pitched forward, dead.

"Come on," said Gunn, passing Yancy, "you'll have to take care of the women. Clarita, let the cavalry handle it."

Clarita looked up at him, and rose to her feet. They walked toward the horses as the cavalry rode past, shooting stragglers, returning fire to those Apaches who still fought from horseback.

Gunn caught up Esquire, and sheathed his Winchester.

"Where are you going?" asked Janice.

"There's a price on my head," he replied. "Right or wrong. If the army gets me, I'm liable to hang."

"Where will you go?"

"I'll look you up if I'm ever in California."

"But I love you, Gunn!"

Gunn hauled himself into the saddle.

Major Heller, Captain Rice, and their aides rode up. Gunn kicked Esquire in the flanks and rode past them. He tipped his hat in farewell.

Cavalry troopers surrounded the officers, asking for orders.

"He's getting away, Captain. Want us to run him down?"

"You have your orders," said Heller.

Rice sat there. Yancy, Clarita, Amity, and Janice came walking up to the group of soldiers. Yancy, his face begrimed, saw the soldiers bringing up their rifles.

"He saved these women," said Yancy.

189

"He's wanted for murder," said Rice.

The troopers wheeled their horses, starting to move out.

"Hold up, men," said Rice. "I didn't give the order to take that man."

"But he's gettin' away, Cap'n."

"Let him go," said Rice, staring straight at Heller. "I can't bring a man like that in. I don't care what he did before. What he did here today proves him a better man than most."

Gunn stopped on a low rise to look back.

No one was after him. He lifted his hat and waved it.

Captain Rice saluted him.

Heller frowned, looking at his daughter Amity, then did the same.

"Come on," said Rice, "let's assess the damage. Troopers, to your duty."

The troopers watched the officers ride off around the fire's perimeter.

"He done wrong," said one soldier. "He can get busted for lettin' that outlaw loose."

"Heller might bring charges, at that."

"I wouldn't, was I Heller. I wouldn't want to be the man who did that."

"Boy, that was some shootin', huh?"

"Next to that Gunn feller, we can't shoot for beans. Did you see the hole in that Apache's head? Dead center, Nelson. Dead center."

FORGE AHEAD IN **THE SCOUT** SERIES
BY BUCK GENTRY

#7: PRAIRIE BUSH (1110, $2.50)

Red-headed Melissa, an Army general's daughter, is in good hands with the Scout. And when they learn that her father has been kidnapped, she offers to help the Scout in any way she can—making this Holten's most sizzling adventure ever!

#8: PAWNEE RAMPAGE (1161, $2.50)

When the Scout finds himself at war with the entire Pawnee nation—to avenge the death of his Sioux bride—who can blame him for finding solace in the arms of a sumptuous lady journalist who's doing a piece on the frontier?

#9: APACHE AMBUSH (1193, $2.50)

Eli Holten has his hands full while scouting for a wagon train down the Santa Fe trail: his client runs the most famous "sporting house" in St. Louis, and she's moving it—lock, stock, and twenty girls!

#10: TRAITOR'S GOLD (1209, $2.50)

There's a luscious red-head who's looking for someone to lead her through the Black Hills of the Dakotas. And one look at the Scout tells her she's found her man—for whatever job she has in mind!

Available wherever paperbacks are sold, or order direct from the Publisher. Send cover price plus 50¢ per copy for mailing and handling to Zebra Books, 475 Park Avenue South, New York, N.Y. 10016 DO NOT SEND CASH.